# Christopher Pike

# Chain Letter 2
## The Ancient Evil

**AN ARCHWAY PAPERBACK**
Published by POCKET BOOKS

New York   London   Toronto   Sydney   Tokyo   Singapore

AN ARCHWAY PAPERBACK *Original*

An Archway Paperback published by
POCKET BOOKS, a division of Simon & Schuster Inc.
1230 Avenue of the Americas, New York, NY 10020

ISBN: 0-671-74506-9

First Archway Paperback printing April 1992

10  9  8  7  6  5  4  3

AN ARCHWAY PAPERBACK and colophon are registered trademarks of Simon & Schuster Inc.

Cover art by Brian Kotzky

Printed in the U.S.A.

IL 8+

# THE CHAIN LETTER

*My Dearest,*

*You thought you knew me, but you did not. You thought I was your friend, but I am not. I am the real Caretaker, and I am going to take care of you. Listen closely.*

*At the bottom of this communication is a list of names. Your name is at the top. What is required of you—at present—is a small token of obedience. After you have performed this small service, you will remove your name from Column III and place it in the box. Once you are in the box, you will stay in the box. Then you will make a copy of this communication and mail it to the individual now at the top of Column III. The specifics of the small service you are to perform will be listed in the classified ads of the* Times *under Personals —in backward code. The individual following you on the list must receive this letter within three days of today.*

*Feel free to discuss this communication with others on the list. Like myself, they are not your friends, but they do know all your sins. Do not discuss this communication with anyone outside the group. If you do, you will anger me.*

*If you do not perform the small service listed in the paper or if you break the chain of this communication, you will be horribly killed.*

*Sincerely,*
*Your Caretaker*

**Books by Christopher Pike**

BURY ME DEEP
CHAIN LETTER 2: THE ANCIENT EVIL
DIE SOFTLY
FALL INTO DARKNESS
FINAL FRIENDS #1: THE PARTY
FINAL FRIENDS #2: THE DANCE
FINAL FRIENDS #3: THE GRADUATION
GIMME A KISS
LAST ACT
MASTER OF MURDER
MONSTER
REMEMBER ME
ROAD TO NOWHERE
SCAVENGER HUNT
SEE YOU LATER
SPELLBOUND
WHISPER OF DEATH
WITCH

Available from ARCHWAY Paperbacks

*For Neil*

# Chain Letter 2
## The Ancient Evil

# PROLOGUE

The chain letter came as it had before. First to Fran Darey—in a purple envelope with no return address. It came totally out of the blue, and like the original letter, it carried with it a threat of danger. And like before, at first no one listened.

Until it was too late.

Fran Darey was just returning home from a morning of hard work when she collected the mail. Summer was almost over and so was her job at the local mall. She worked at the McDonald's, and although it would be fair to say she did not hate her job, it would also have been fair to say she was never going to work in a fast-food joint again. The job didn't allow her to use her full physical and mental potential. Heck, she was going to college in a few weeks. She was going to get straight A's and graduate in four years and make the world a better place. She was never going to have to worry how many more fries there were in a big scoop versus a medium scoop—a question she had been asked three times that day by smart-mouthed junior high kids.

But too soon Fran would have wished to have such mundane problems.

A strange thing happened as Fran reached to remove the mail from her parents' mailbox. Even before she touched or saw the purple envelope, she thought of Neil Hurly. She had of course thought of Neil many times over the course of the summer, since he had died of a horrible cancer. But no thought had ever come to her so strong. A cold sweat rose on the back of her neck, and a tear formed in the corner of one eye. She had loved Neil, she thought, and she had never told him. She couldn't imagine what could be worse in life. Never once, in the weeks following the incident with the chain letter, had she blamed him for what had happened. He had been sick, after all. He had not been evil.

"Miss you," Fran whispered under her breath. She almost turned and glanced over her shoulder right then, his presence was so strong. He could have been standing right behind her.

It was a pity he wasn't. He might have stopped her hand.

Fran reached inside the box and took out the mail. She noticed the purple envelope immediately.

*No, Jesus, no,* she thought.

Her heart almost stopped. But her hands did not. Dropping all the other letters and bills and assorted junk mail, her fingers tore into the purple envelope and pulled out the letter inside. She began to read.

*My Dearest,*
  *You thought you knew me, but you did not. You thought I was your friend, but I am not. I am the real Caretaker, and I am going to take care of you. Listen closely. . . .*

Standing alone outside her house, Fran screamed. Her throat was tight; the sound came out pitifully thin and high. It was doubtful her nearest neighbor could have heard. But the sound of her scream was to echo over the next few days, until it became a full-fledged wail. Her scream was the beginning, if the chain of the letters could be said to have a beginning—or an end.

# CHAPTER ONE

At the time the second wave of chain letters began, Tony Hunt and Alison Parker were trying to decide whether to make love or never speak to each other again. The situation was filled with contradictions. They were alone in Alison's house. Her parents were not going to be home for several hours. Neither of them was a virgin. In fact, they were each responsible for their mutual lack of virginity. They had been true to each other the few months they had been dating. They were both healthy, and in a sense they were both willing. But neither of them was happy. That was the main contradiction.

Alison thought the problem was Tony's fault, and although Tony was normally not one to place blame, he thought it was Alison's fault. It was she, after all, who had decided to go to college three thousand miles away instead of thirty. The situation had arisen only the previous week when Alison had received a rather surprisingly late invitation to attend NYU to study drama. That was New York University in New York City, on the other side of the country from UCLA, where Alison had been planning to go. Alison had already called the airlines. It took a modern jet five hours to get to New York. For Tony that was an awful long way to have his girl fly. He was going to miss her—boy, was he going to.

But Tony was not unreasonable. He could understand that it was a wonderful opportunity for Alison. She had initially applied to NYU and been turned down because the competition to get in their highly rated drama department was unbelievable. He knew there would be great teachers in New York, and she would learn great things. Yet he also knew that UCLA had an excellent drama department, and that when all things were factored in and set down in two lists—one of pros and one of cons—the fact that he was in Los Angeles, and not in New York, should have been a major factor. And that was why he was upset. Because Alison was acting as if she couldn't understand why he was upset. She was acting as if she didn't care.

He hoped she was acting. He really did love her, more than he liked to admit to himself.

At present Alison was pacing back and forth between the kitchen and the living room, wearing a towel on her head and a towel around her midsection and nothing else. She often paced when she was angry. Lately she had been wearing out the carpet. He was still fully dressed, but if they hadn't started fighting, he would have been in bed with her by now. That was another thing that bugged him. She was mad that he hadn't *at least* waited until they had had sex to bring up her relocation venture. Golly, he thought, wasn't that uncool of him. He didn't have one of those push-button physiologies they wrote about in *Cosmopolitan*. He couldn't be intimate when his mind was going ten thousand miles an hour. He wasn't a space shuttle, for godsake. But turmoil was no obstacle to her.

"We can talk all we want while I'm away," Alison said. "There are things called phones. People all over the world use them to stay close to the ones they love."

Tony grunted. "I've heard about them. You have to put quarters in them to talk to the other side of the country. Lots of quarters."

"You can call me collect, I don't care."

"You can then send the bill to me, I don't care," Tony said. "Neither of us will have the money to pay it."

"We don't have to talk that much," Alison said.

"You mean, we don't have to stay that close?"

Alison finally sat on the couch beside him and angrily crossed her legs. The towel on her head was white. The other was pink. It went well with her very tan legs. She glared at him.

"I don't understand why you're trying to make me feel guilty," she said.

"I'm not trying to make you feel guilty."

"Yes, you are."

"No, I'm not."

"You are."

He shrugged. "All right."

"Don't just say all right. Answer me. Why are you doing this to me?"

Tony threw up his hands in frustration. "What am I

7

doing to you? You're doing it to me. You're leaving me. I'm not leaving you. You have it backward."

Alison put on her patient face, which at the moment was a mask of poorly concealed exasperation. But he couldn't help enjoying her expression, maybe because it belonged to her. Her beauty was unusual, her features at odds with one another, but in a way that somehow brought them together into a whole that was greater than its parts. Her big eyes and her wide mouth were classics. The rest of her, though—her button nose and thick eyebrows—was supposed to be out of style. That was what *Cosmopolitan* would say. But Alison always had style. She had enough for the next sixty years, in his opinion.

*And now her style will have a New York flavor.*

Her only physical flaw was her left arm. It was badly scarred from her battle with Neil.

"We wouldn't be three thousand miles apart if you had accepted that football scholarship to Harvard," Alison said with exaggerated patience. "That was your choice, not mine. Harvard would have been just up the road. I refuse to accept full responsibility for this separation."

"Harvard offered me that scholarship seven months ago," Tony said dryly. "Nobody was going to New York seven months ago. Nobody was even going together then."

Alison tapped his leg as if she had just received a brilliant idea. "I bet they still want you! Why don't you give them a call? We can call them right now." She stood. "I'll get their number from Information."

He grabbed her arm, stopping her. "Harvard's

football team is probably practicing as we speak. I can't just call them and tell them I want to be their next starting quarterback." He let go of her arm. "Besides, I told you, I don't want to play anymore."

She was impatient. "Why not? You're a gifted athlete. How many people are born with an arm like yours? Your talent can open up whole worlds for you. God gave you your abilities to use, not to run away from."

Now she was cutting low. She knew why he didn't want to play football anymore. In the middle of his fabulous senior season, he'd hurt his back. At first it had seemed like no big deal. In fact, he'd even gone out for track and done well. But backs were funny, his doctor told him. You could injure them and not feel the full impact of the injury for several months. Shortly after graduation and Neil's death, he started to wake up in the middle of the night in pain. It was mainly in his lower back, but if he turned the wrong way in bed or bent over too far during the day, the pain would shoot into his legs like burning needles slipped into his nerves. He was presently seeing a chiropractor three times a week, and that was helping. The chiropractor thought he'd heal up just fine, as long as he avoided being crunched by two-hundred-and-fifty-pound linemen. But Alison thought chiropractors were quacks, and she often hinted that his injury might be psychosomatic. Yeah, right, he thought sarcastically, it was all in his head. Somebody should tell his back that.

But sometimes Tony wondered if his pain was *indirectly* related to Neil's death. He often thought about Neil when he lay awake at night. Supposedly time healed grief, but if that was true, time was taking its sweet time. He missed Neil as much as he had the day Neil died.

But sometimes he felt as if Neil were still right there, beside him. Like a hovering angel. He would turn suddenly and expect to catch Neil's sweet sad smile. Of course he never did. It was all just wishful thinking.

"It seems to me," Tony said softly, "that we've talked for hours about why I don't want to play anymore. I'm sure you remember. It has something to do with my back."

"How do you know your back just doesn't need a little exercise?" Alison asked.

"Having your vertebrae pulverized by oncoming helmets does not constitute exercise."

Alison shook herself and almost lost one of her towels. "Why is it we can't talk without you getting sarcastic? You never used to be this way."

"I guess this is just the way I am." Tony was suddenly tired of the argument. "What do you want to do? If you want to go to New York—go. I won't stop you."

"But you will make me feel guilty about it. You don't mind doing that."

Tony shrugged. "I guess I'm just feeling sorry for myself."

"Why?"

Tony looked right at her. A wet curl of her long dark hair hung over her right cheek, near her eye. He reached out and brushed it away, and for a moment he touched her soft skin and a thousand gentle memories flooded his mind. But he didn't let his touch linger because the memories only made him sad.

"Because I'm going to miss you," he told her. "I'm going to miss you more than I can stand."

She softened slightly. "I'm going to miss you, too, Tony. You know that."

He continued to stare at her. She was so beautiful. She would be just as beautiful in New York. The guys there would surely agree.

"You'll meet someone else," he said.

She was offended. "That's ridiculous."

"It's reality. You're young. You're pretty. I'll be on the other side of the country." He nodded. "It'll happen—sooner than you think."

She stood, mad. "You don't put much stock in my loyalty, do you? What do you think I am, a slut? I can't believe you just said what you did. You have some nerve."

Tony wondered if he had said too much. The problem was—he had just spoken his mind honestly. All during high school girls had pursued him. He had no false modesty about his good looks. He was a blond, blue-eyed, all-American boy, built like a stud. Alison had chased after him at first, too, but now that she was suddenly leaving, it was he who was attached. The experience was new to him, and he hated it. The thought of her dating other guys plagued him like a virus, and he couldn't be free of it. If he imagined her kissing another guy, he would actually become sick to his stomach.

And what made it all worse was that he *was* being

realistic. Long-distance romances just didn't work, not when you were eighteen years old. She would meet new guys in New York, and that would be the end of Tony and Alison. In a way he was getting what he deserved. He had, after all, stolen Alison from Neil.

*But that's not true. Neil and Alison were never a couple, except in Neil's head.*

Then again, maybe he and Alison were only a couple in his head.

"You're not a slut," he said and sighed. "I'm sorry said what I did."

She continued to stand. "You're trying to hurt me."

"I'm not. I said I was sorry."

"It's a great opportunity for me."

"I understand that."

"Then why can't you be happy for me?" she asked.

"I am happy for you. I'm just more unhappy for me. And I can't understand— Oh, never mind." He stood. "I should go."

It was her turn to stop him. "No. Say what you were going to say."

"It was nothing."

"I want to hear it. What can't you understand?"

Tony looked at her once more. The towel on her head had shifted to the right side and now there was a whole handful of wet hair he could brush away. But he couldn't bear to touch her again. If he did, he knew he wouldn't be able to leave, and he had to get away. It was better to end things between them now—so she wouldn't have to dump him later with a Dear John letter.

"I can't understand how you can just leave me," he

said. When she began to protest, he raised his hand. "No. Let's not argue anymore. It's the difference between us. I would never leave you."

Alison's eyes moistened, and she clenched her hands in frustration. "I love you just as much as you love me. How can you say that?"

He shook his head. "I've got to go." He turned away. "Have fun in New York."

She called to him as he walked toward the door, and by now she was crying openly. "What's that supposed to mean? You're going for good? I don't leave for another two weeks. You're not even going to come back to say goodbye? Tony!"

He paused at the door, keeping his back to her. "You can do what you want," he said. "You have my permission."

"I'm not going to do anything!" she cried, moving closer. "I love you. I just want to be with you."

He glanced over his shoulder. "Then stay, Ali. Stay."

Her face was a mess of tears. Yet she was also wearing her old friend—her pride. Alison was a proud girl. He had recognized that about her not long after they had met. She wanted to be an actress. No, she wanted to be a famous actress. She wanted admirers. He'd had those once. He'd been the toast of the town when he'd led their high school team to the city championship. But being popular had meant nothing to him. Certainly it had not been worth the price of a bad back. That was another difference between them. Another reason why he should break it off now. Her tearful face was suddenly not so soft.

"I have to go," she said.

"Then go," he said. He opened the door. "Good bye."

"Tony!"

He let the door close behind him without answering her. Had he paused on the porch, he might not have been able to leave. But he didn't pause, and the chain of letters had fertile ground to begin again.

# CHAPTER TWO

*T*hat same afternoon Alison Parker had a date with Brenda Paxson to go shopping for clothes for Alison —warm things to wear in the cold East Coast fall and winter. That morning Alison had had fun planning the stores they would visit and the money they would spend. Alison's mother had given her a gold credit card with the dangerous instruction to buy what she needed. To Alison that was the next thing to heaven.

Yet as Alison drove toward Brenda's house, she was far from a happy camper. She was dismayed by Tony's reaction to her leaving. She thought he was being immature about the whole matter. He wasn't acting at all like the guy she had fallen in love with. That Tony had been as cool as an unlit candle and as secure as a rock. This new guy was clinging to her like an emotional cripple. Sure, he was going to miss her. She was going to miss him. But life was like that. People had to go their separate ways sometimes. It didn't mean they had to break up. God, she hoped not. She wasn't interested in anybody except Tony. Even when he was in one of his moods, he was still pretty right on, and he was the only guy she had ever really cared about. She had been dying to hold him earlier, but he had walked out on her. He could be really weird at times.

Brenda was standing outside her house, watering the lawn, when Alison drove up. She had a red bow in her shiny blond hair and ass-kissing black shorts that showed off her lithe figure. She seemed to be happy, and Alison hoped she was. Brenda wouldn't be starting college with the rest of them. Her parents were having financial difficulties, and she had to work to help out. She was currently employed by a shipping company and making good money. She didn't seem to mind the work, and Alison wondered if Brenda wasn't relieved to be taking a break from studying. Brenda had never been one to hit the books.

"You're early," Brenda called, throwing down the running hose on the lawn. "I haven't had a chance to change."

Alison climbed out of her car and brushed her hair back. It was a warm day, but windy. It had taken her an hour to drive to her friend's house from her own. They had grown up around the block from each other, but Alison's family moved to a new housing tract just weeks before the two girls graduated from high school. The tract had been practically deserted back in June, and it had been there that Neil, in the guise of the Caretaker, had attacked her.

*Poor Neil,* she thought. He'd been so sick at the time.

Better not think about him. She knew Tony still did, which was probably a big part of his problem with her leaving. Neil had been Tony's best friend, and best friends were not easy to replace.

"You're dressed as well as you want to be," Alison said, walking toward her own best friend. "You love nothing better than sliding around the mall scantily clad."

Brenda turned off the hose. "Really, Ali, I think I have more dignity than that."

"If you do, you keep it well hidden."

Brenda wiped her hands on her shorts and reached for her sneakers, which were sitting on the front porch. "And what was Miss Conservative doing just before she drove over to pick up her loose friend? Enjoying carnal pleasures with her boyfriend perhaps?"

Alison felt her face fall, although she tried her best to hold it up. "No," she said softly. "Not really."

Brenda was instantly alert to the change in her tone. "Did you and Tony have a fight?" she asked, concerned.

Alison put a hand to her head. It was handy place for it—a moment later she was wiping away a tear. "He's mad at me," Alison said sadly. "I don't know— maybe I shouldn't leave. In a way I don't want to."

"That's nonsense," Brenda said, slinging an arm around her friend's shoulder. "Going to NYU is a dream come true for you. Tony's just got to grow up and understand that he doesn't own you."

"But he's right, I could go to UCLA. They have a fine drama department, and then we could still see each other." She sniffed. "Maybe I am only thinking of myself."

"You have to think about yourself," Brenda said, turning once more for her shoes. "Now, I'm going to say something and don't take it wrong. What if you do decide to stay here, and Tony and you break up in six months?"

"We're not going to break up," Alison said quickly.

"But what if you do? People do, you know. Then what? You'll be mad as hell at Tony and yourself for ruining your big chance. You'll have thrown it away and gotten nothing in return. Take my advice, sister, and go to New York and find a new boyfriend there."

Alison shook her head. "You don't understand. I love Tony."

Brenda sat to tie her shoelaces. "So what? I love Kipp. That doesn't mean I let him run my life. Don't get me wrong. I like Tony. He's a babe, and he's got manners. But we're young. We're going to be in love dozens of times before it's all over."

Alison raised her eyes to peer at the sky, through the thin haze of smog that hung over the city. Everything Brenda said made sense. Yet it felt wrong. Alison lifted an arm to shield her eyes from the glare.

"There's only one sun," Alison said with feeling. "It's always the same, but it's always the best. Do you know what I mean?"

Brenda snickered at the sentiment as she finished her shoes. "Guys are a dime a dozen. They come and go like streetcars."

Alison lowered her hand, her eyes. "Tony's not a streetcar."

Brenda changed the subject. "Fran called. She left a

message on our machine. She said it was vital I call her immediately. Sounds like Fran, huh? Should I call her before we leave?"

"No." Alison sighed. "Let's stop by her house. She might want to come with us."

"All right," Brenda said.

Fran didn't answer the door when Alison and Brenda knocked. When they peeked inside, they were surprised that Fran was sitting at the kitchen table. She should have heard them knocking. The L.A. *Times* lay spread out on the table in front of her.

"Hello?" Brenda said to Fran as Brenda and Alison stepped all the way inside. "Are we in? Are we happy? Is life good?"

Fran didn't answer. She continued to sit with her face buried in her hands. Fran was often overly emotional, so neither Alison nor Brenda was unduly concerned. Alison crossed to the table and touched Fran on the back.

"It can't be that bad," Alison told her.

In response Fran removed her hands from her face and stared at them both with red eyes. Without saying a word, she fished under the paper and withdrew a purple envelope. She held it out with a trembling hand for one of them to take. Alison felt afraid as her eyes fell upon it, even before she realized the envelope was the same color and shape as the ones Neil's chain letters had been sent in. She forced a laugh.

"Don't tell me it's another chain letter?" Alison said.

Fran nodded. Her voice came out like a croak. "Yeah."

"Let me see that thing," Brenda snapped, pulling the letter out of Fran's fingers. She ripped the letter out. Alison peered over Brenda's shoulder, and they read it together.

*My Dearest,*

*You thought you knew me, but you did not. You thought I was your friend, but I am not. I am the real Caretaker, and I am going to take care of you. Listen closely.*

*At the bottom of this communication is a list of names. Your name is at the top. What is required of you—at present—is a small token of obedience. After you have performed this small service, you will remove your name from Column III and place it in the box. Once you are in the box, you will stay in the box. Then you will make a copy of this communication and mail it to the individual now at the top of Column III. The specifics of the small service you are to perform will be listed in the classified ads of the* Times *under Personals—in backward code. The individual following you on the list must receive this letter within three days of today.*

*Feel free to discuss this communication with the others on the list. Like myself, they are not your friends, but they do know all your sins. Do not discuss this communication with anyone outside the group. If you do, you will anger me.*

*If you do not perform the small service listed in*

*the paper or if you break the chain of this commu-
nication, you will be horribly killed.*

> *Sincerely,*
> *Your Caretaker*

*Column III*

*Fran*
*Kipp*
*Brenda*
*Joan*
*Tony*

For a full minute none of them spoke or moved. It
was as it had been a few months earlier. They were in
the same place. They had the same kind of letter in
their hands—the same kind of fear in their hearts. Yet
their fear was different, too. Months ago they'd had no
idea of the horror that would follow the letter. At first
they had thought it might be a joke. Now their fear
was based on bitter experience. Yet it would lead them
to the same conclusion as before. Brenda was the first
to say it out loud.

"This is a bad joke," she said and crumpled up the
letter. Alison stopped her.

"Wait a second," Alison said, taking it out of
Brenda's hands. "I want to study this thing."

"What's there to study?" Brenda asked angrily.
"One of the others sent it to scare us. It was probably
Joan."

"What about Kipp?" Alison asked.

"It could have been Kipp," Brenda was quick to
agree. "What did I tell you about guys? They're a pain

in the ass all around. Let's toss this thing and get to the mall. I'm hungry."

"It's not a joke," Fran whispered.

"Of course it is," Brenda said, sounding as if she were addressing a small child. "Neil's dead. He's not sending any more letters."

Fran nodded to the paper. "There's an ad under Personals in there." Fran trembled. "It's for me."

Alison grabbed the paper. It took her only a second to spot the ad. Fran had worked out the code on the empty column beside it. The original ad read: NARFTHGINOTYPPUPRUOYNWORD. Decoded it said:

Drown your puppy tonight, Fran.

Alison's face twisted in disgust. "This is sick. Kipp wouldn't place an ad like this."

Brenda glanced at it and shook her head. "It must have been Joan, then. Anybody who dresses like her has got to be sick."

"But Joan likes animals," Alison said. "She has a dog. She wouldn't want Fran to drown her puppy."

Brenda was getting exasperated. "Of course Joan doesn't expect Fran to drown her puppy. She knows Fran isn't that stupid. She's just trying to scare us. She has to say something weird."

Alison stared once more at the letter. It was neatly typed, as Neil's had been. It was not a photocopy. "I don't know," she muttered.

Brenda lost her temper. "What don't you know? The wording and ideas of this letter are almost identical to the ones Neil sent us. The person who sent this couldn't even be bothered thinking up something original. It has to be someone in the group. We're the only ones who knew about the chain letters."

"Will you quit yelling at me," Alison said.

"I am not yelling at you!" Brenda yelled.

"Yes, you are," Fran said.

"Well, if I am it's your fault," Brenda yelled at Fran. "Why didn't you throw this thing away when you got it and not bother us with it? We've got stuff to do. We've got to go shopping."

Alison sat down at the table, studying the column of names at the bottom. "How come I'm not on this list?" she asked.

"It doesn't matter who's there," Brenda said impatiently.

"I think it does," Alison said. "If someone in the group was trying to play a joke on us, then he or she would have known to include my name. They would have known that I had been involved before."

"Are you saying that the person who sent this letter doesn't know exactly what happened before?" Fran asked.

"I think it's possible," Alison said, and the possibility filled her with dread. If someone outside their group knew even a little about what had happened the summer before, then they were in hot water. After all, they had accidentally run over a man in the desert.

At least, they thought they had run over him. They had been driving blind at night, with their lights out. For all they knew, the man could have been lying dead when they hit him. The man had had no wallet. They had never even been able to identify him. But one thing was for sure, they had buried him, and they

23

hadn't told the police about it, and that was a punisha
ble crime.

"Doesn't this discussion strike any of you as famil
iar?" Brenda asked. "We had it a couple of month
ago. We thought the letter must be from someone i
the group, but then we figured it couldn't be one of u
'cause it was too weird. Well, it turned out to be Neil
and he was with us that night. It'll be the same thi
time."

"Are you saying someone else in the group has gon
insane?" Fran asked.

"Yes," Brenda said. "You and Alison for believin,
this garbage."

Alison stood. "We have to call the others. Let's cal
Kipp and Tony."

"I'd call Joan first myself," Brenda said. "She'l
probably bust up laughing."

"I don't want to call Joan," Alison said. Tony had
gone out a few times with Joan before he had startec
to date her. Joan had never forgiven her for stealin;
the guy she considered to be her boyfriend. It was al
absurd—Tony said he hadn't even made out witl
Joan.

Alison set the letter beside the phone and dialec
Tony's number. She got his machine. She didn't leave
a message. She tried Kipp's number. Tony had saic
something earlier about going over to see Kipp. Bu
she got Kipp's machine as well. She left a message fo
him to call her at Fran's house as soon as he got in. She
didn't say anything about the chain letter. For all she
knew his parents might listen to his messages. She

called Tony back and left a similar message on his machine. Then, reluctantly, she tried Joan. She got another answering machine. The world was full of them. She left a message for Joan to call them at Fran's ASAP.

"I think we should wait here until we get one of them on the phone," Alison said, setting the receiver down.

"What?" Brenda complained. "We're going to blow out the rest of day because of a stupid letter? Give me a break. If you're not going to the mall, I am. Give me your car keys."

"No," Alison said. "You're going to shut up and sit here and wait with Fran and me. This letter may be a joke. It probably is. But it might be serious, and if it is, we have to stick together. That's what we learned last time. All right?"

Brenda sat down with a big huff. "I didn't learn anything last time—except to stay away from the mailbox."

It may have been a coincidence, or the dog may have been psychic and known he was being discussed. In either case, Fran's puppy suddenly ran into the kitchen and began to lick his master's hands. Fran reached down and patted the cute little brown cocker spaniel on the head. An anxious smile touched her lips.

"It must be a joke," Fran said. "No one could want Barney dead. No one could think I'd actually drown him."

"I'm sure you're right," Alison replied. But a chill

25

went through her as she thought about what Fran had just said. Alison stared at the letter again. The *small service* was absolutely unthinkable. Perhaps this Caretaker wasn't the least bit interested in seeing Barney dead. Maybe he was only interested in having an excuse to harm Fran.

# CHAPTER THREE

*T*ony Hunt didn't leave Alison Parker's house and drive straight to Kipp's. He stopped at the mall near his house first. He was hungry, and there were a dozen different places to eat there. Also, at the back of his mind, he hoped to *accidentally* run into Alison, who was supposed to go shopping with Brenda. He thought this was pretty ironic since he had just walked out on Alison. But he was beginning to accept as normal the contradictions between his thoughts and his actions. Nowadays his whole existence seemed one vast vat of confusion.

Tony didn't know what was wrong with himself. Alison was leaving town, of course, but if he was completely honest with himself, he had to admit that he had been feeling anxious even before her invitation from NYU arrived. He tried to rationalize that the pain in his back must be throwing him off more than he realized. Yet he had been hurt before and hadn't lost his sense of inner stability. As he examined his feelings, the clearer it became that his sense of confusion and foreboding had started with the arrival of Neil's chain letter. Yet his anxiety hadn't culminated with Neil's death and then begun to heal. It continued even now to hang over his head. He missed Neil terribly, sure, but why the continuing feelings of anxiety and foreboding? Why not simply sorrow and loneliness? Those emotions would have been natural and easily explainable. It was almost as if nothing had ended with Neil's death, except Neil.

Tony parked in the warm sun and walked into the mall. The cool air and shopper sounds enfolded him like a hug. He liked malls, which was odd because he seldom bought anything. But he could walk around in a mall for an hour and just observe people—so preoccupied with their latest purchases, so delighted with the silliest little things. He watched them but always felt separate from them. In fact, he felt closer to the mannequins in the windows. The silent observers. Hadn't that been a line from Neil's chain letter? *I am the Observer, the Recorder. I am also the Punisher.* Tony felt as if he were still being punished for a crime he wasn't even sure he had committed. This was another feeling that had only begun in the last few months, long after they had buried the man in the desert.

Tony went to the food circle. His tastes were uncreative. He ordered a hamburger, fries, and a Coke from the McDonald's—he figured he couldn't go wrong with that. He had hoped Fran Darey might be working. The cashier told him that Fran had already left for the day. Fran was a high-strung worrywart, but she always had a smile and a kind word for him. Tony could hardly remember the last time Alison had looked happy to see him. God, girls changed when you got to know them. They turned into people with problems. People who wanted you to solve their problems.

Tony took his food into the center of the tables and sat beside the good-luck fountain, where for a tossed penny and a silent prayer all your wishes might come true. Tony pulled a nickel from his pocket and threw it into the splashing water. It was a good throw; it landed on the top circular tier. Alison was right—he had a hell of an arm. But no wish came to his mind, only the desire that his unhappiness be gone. He picked up his hamburger and took a bite. They had cooked it well done, just the way he liked it. A soft laugh sounded to his right.

"I make a wish every day at this time," a girl said. "I don't know if they don't come true because I don't know what I want or because I only use a penny."

Tony looked over and was surprised to see a beautiful young woman at the next table. Her hair was long and shiny, an odd maroon so deep red it was almost black. Her green eyes shone bright above her thick lips, which were painted a warm red. Her face was pale, but cute freckles played around her shapely nose and her innocent dimples. She was drinking a cup of coffee and reading a magazine. Her dress was entirely white, like that of a nurse. She smiled as his eyes met hers, and he found himself smiling in return.

"Maybe we should use quarters," he said.

She nodded. "Then we could do a month's worth of wishing in one throw."

He gestured around them. "You come here a lot?"

"For lunch, yeah. I work near here. At the hospital."

"What do you do?"

She made a face. "Today I'm drawing blood. Exciting, huh?"

"You don't like your job?"

She shrugged. "It's a job. It pays the bills. What do you do?"

He didn't want to sound as if he'd just graduated from high school. He put her age at about twenty-one, two years older than he was. "I'm in college," he muttered.

"I was in college once. Where do you go?"

It was his plan to attend a local junior college for the first two years. Without an athletic scholarship, he couldn't afford anything else. But he gave Alison's first choice of schools because it sounded more impressive. He didn't know why he wanted to impress this girl. It wasn't normally his style.

"UCLA," he said.

"That's where I went to school! It's a neat campus, isn't it?"

"I like it."

"What's your major?" she asked. She had a wonderful voice. It conveyed warmth and excitement at the same time.

"I'd like to be a teacher," he said. "But I haven't settled on a definite major."

"It's a bitch having to choose, isn't it? I'm not even

in school, and I'm still changing my major." She nodded to his food. "Your hamburger's getting cold. I should leave you alone and let you eat."

Tony paused. She was right. He should finish his food and get on with his day. Kipp would be waiting for him. But he suddenly realized he was enjoying himself, chatting with this stranger about odds and ends. He used to have fun with Alison like this, back when they could communicate.

"I can eat and talk at the same time," he said. "What's your name?"

"Sasha." She offered her hand across the five feet that separated them. "What's yours?"

"Tony Hunt." He shook her hand. Her skin was soft, like Alison's, but her grip was firm. "I'm pleased to meet you, Sasha."

She smiled again. Her teeth were a little crooked, but still nice. "You know, you look kind of familiar," she said. "Have I seen you before?"

He suspected she had seen his picture in the papers, extolling his accomplishments on the football field. He didn't want to tell her that, though. Then she would know he had just graduated. Besides, she might want to talk about football, and nothing bored him more.

"You might have seen me here," he said. "I come here often enough."

"I suppose." She frowned slightly. "Is there something wrong with your neck or your back?"

She had caught him off guard. "Why do you ask?"

"The way you hold yourself. You look stiff."

31

His chiropractor had been able to spot the problem just by looking at him, but no one else had ever commented on it before. Sasha must be a very perceptive young woman, he thought.

"It's an old sports injury," he said. "It flares up every now and then."

"I'm considering being a physical therapist," Sasha said. "I'll have to go back to school to get certified, but I've been studying a lot on my own about deep-tissue massage. You should get a massage. It can give tremendous relief."

Tony smiled shyly but spoke boldly. "If you ever want someone to practice on, give me a call."

Sasha surprised him. "I could give you a massage." She reached for her purse. "You can give me a call if you want one."

Tony shifted uncomfortably in his seat. Although he was pleased that he might be seeing Sasha again, guilt weighed heavy on him. If Alison had solicited the number of another guy, and he caught her, he would have been furious. On the other hand, he thought, Alison would probably be giving out her number soon enough—in New York. Besides, it wasn't like he was making a date with Sasha. She was just going to give him a massage. . . .

"That's very nice of you," he said. "I wouldn't mind trying it— What did you call it?"

"A deep-tissue massage." She scribbled down her number on a scrap of paper and handed it to him. "It was nice to meet you, Tony." She grabbed her purse and stood up. "Call me any evening. I'm usually home."

He studied her number. It was local. He stood to say goodbye to her. "It was nice meeting you, Sasha."

She smiled one last time and tapped him lightly on the shoulder as she turned away. She had a sweet smile, innocent and carefree.

"Later," she said.

"Yeah, sure," he replied. He watched as she disappeared in the crowd. He had been so enchanted with her voice and face, he had hardly noticed her excellent figure, much fuller than Alison's.

*Enchanted.*

There had been something enchanting about Sasha. Tony looked once more at the number in his hand and stuffed it in his pocket. He left the mall without finishing his lunch.

Kipp Coughlan was pulling into his driveway when Tony Hunt arrived at his house. Tony parked behind him and got out of his car.

"I'm glad you weren't waiting for me," Tony said.

"Were you here earlier?" Kipp asked, his expression good-natured as usual. He had fair hair, a big nose, and even bigger ears, which made him appear silly. But his dark eyes were sharp, and so was his mind. Kipp was heading for MIT in a couple of weeks to study aeronautical engineering. He had been the class valedictorian.

"No. I stopped at the mall for a bite," Tony said.

"Too bad, I was hoping we could eat together." Kipp walked toward his front door, a brown paper bag in his hand. "I'm watching Leslie."

Leslie was Kipp's little sister. They were devoted to

each other. She was seven years old and every bit as smart as her brother.

"Did you go out and leave her alone?" Tony asked, following Kipp into the house. Kipp gestured to the bag he was carrying.

"I had to," Kipp said. "She found an injured bird in the backyard. Its wing is broken. A cat might have got hold of it. Anyway, she ordered me to go get it birdseed while she tended to it. She said if she left the bird, it would die."

Just then Leslie appeared in the living room. She didn't have her brother's ears, but she had his nose. She could best be described as charming rather than pretty. Her fair hair was the same shade as Kipp's, and they had similar mannerisms, the most noticeable being the tendency to talk with their hands when they were excited. Leslie was excited now. She hurried to collect the birdseed.

"Hi, Tony," she said. "Did Kipp tell you about the bird with the broken wing that flew in my window?"

"Yes," Tony said, glancing at Kipp and smiling. "He told me you were nursing it back to health. That's kind of you—helping the poor thing."

"Did you get the baby bird kind?" Leslie asked Kipp as she peered into the bag.

"I didn't know baby birds ate different food from big birds," Kipp said. He gave the bag to his sister. "I bet the bird doesn't know the difference, either."

"I bet he does," Leslie said seriously, running off with the bag.

"Cute," Tony said, watching her go.

"Yeah. Too bad we can't bottle it and sell it." Kipp headed for the stairs. "Did you see Alison today?"

"Yeah."

"How was it?"

"How was what?" Tony asked, following him up to the second floor.

"The sex."

"We didn't have sex."

"Why not?" Kipp asked.

"We don't have sex every time we get together. I'm sure you and Brenda don't, either."

"Yeah, but we have an excuse."

"What's that?" Tony asked.

"Brenda isn't attracted to me."

They entered Kipp's bedroom. Tony noticed the blinking red light on Kipp's answering machine. He also noticed the faded bloodstain on the carpet. When Neil, in his Caretaker craziness, had abducted Kipp, he had soaked the bed and surrounding area with blood. Only later had they learned that the blood had been Neil's, slowly siphoned from his veins over a period of time. It still boggled Tony that Neil, in his weakened condition, had had the strength to kidnap Kipp. Neil had done a lot of amazing things back during the days of the chain letters—some were almost supernatural.

"I'm always happy when I come in my room and see that someone's called me," Kipp said, reaching for the answering machine. "Usually it's just Brenda or you or somebody trying to sell me life insurance. But just before I check the messages, I always have a hope that a gorgeous babe has seen me on the street, somehow found out my number, and has called to ask me out. I don't know why I never stop hoping."

"Aren't you and Brenda getting along?" Tony asked, sitting on the edge of the bed.

"We're going through a rough period right now."

"Any particular reason?"

"I think it's because she doesn't like me anymore."

"I know the feeling," Tony mumbled.

Kipp was surprised. He paused with his hand above the button on the answering machine. "Is Ali still going to New York?"

"Looks like it."

"What a bitch. You're better off without her."

"I guess," Tony said miserably. He shook his head. "Doesn't it depress you when Brenda acts like she doesn't care?"

"No. I'm used to it. It depresses me when she doesn't want to have sex. But I'm getting used to that, too. Just a second, let's see who called."

Kipp played his messages. There was only one. It was from Alison, and she sounded worried. She wanted Kipp to call her at Fran's house as soon as he got in. Kipp looked at Tony for an explanation. Tony didn't have one.

"I don't think it has anything to do with me," Tony said.

"Don't you want to call her instead of me?" Kipp asked.

"No."

"Come on."

"No, I don't," Tony said. "Honestly."

"What did you two fight about today?"

"Her leaving. My not wanting to play football anymore. Our sex life. Her wanting to date other guys."

"She wants to date other guys? Alison? Did she say that?"

"Not exactly," Tony admitted.

"I don't believe it. Forget what I said a moment ago about her being a bitch. Alison's a great girl. There's something special when you two are together. There's a kind of magic in the air."

"There won't be any magic in a couple of weeks. She'll be gone."

Kipp came over and sat beside Tony on the bed. He put his hand on his shoulder. "Hey, buddy, you sound really bummed about this."

Tony nodded weakly. "I am. I'm embarrassed by the way I feel because I've never felt this way before. I just feel like if she goes I'll lose her forever."

"It won't happen. I'm your friend and I'm leaving, but I'm still going to be your friend. Alison will be, too. She loves you. Anyone can see it."

Tony barely smiled. Before the chain letter began, he and Kipp hadn't been real close. Now Kipp was his best friend. There was nothing like a shared trauma to bring people together. He appreciated what Kipp was saying. The trouble was, he didn't believe it. Alison was attracted to him. She had fun with him. She might even have been attached to him, but she didn't love him. You didn't leave the one you love, not for any reason.

"We'll see" was all Tony could say.

"You sure you don't want to call her at Fran's?" Kipp asked. "She does sound upset."

Tony shrugged. "I guess it wouldn't hurt." Tony reached for the phone. "Do you know Fran's number?"

"It's button number six."

Tony pushed the appropriate button. The phone rang only once before it was picked up by Fran. "Hello?" she said.

"Fran, this is Tony. Is Alison there?"

"Yeah."

"Could I speak to her?" Fran was slow in answering. "Is there something wrong?" Tony asked.

"Here's Ali," Fran said finally. Tony listened while the phone shifted hands. Alison came on the line. Her tone of voice was low.

"Where are you, Tony?" she asked.

"I'm at Kipp's house."

"Is Kipp there?"

"Yeah. He's sitting beside me. What's wrong?"

Alison paused. "I don't know how to say this."

Tony's heart pounded loudly in his own ears. Here it came—the big goodbye. We had some good times, Tony, but you're right. I should date other guys. I should have a variety of lovers. You just don't satisfy me anymore. Not like this guy I met this afternoon. Boy, does he have all the right stuff. I'll always love you, Tony, but you know a girl always says that when she's dumping a guy for another guy.

"Just say it," he whispered.

"Tony?"

"I'm here. Say it."

There was another long pause. "Somebody's sent us another chain letter."

Tony couldn't comprehend what she was saying for a moment. "What?" he asked.

"Fran got another chain letter in the mail this morning. It's a lot like the ones Neil sent. If Kipp's there, ask him if he sent it." Her voice was almost trembling. "Tell him it's not funny."

Tony put his hand over the phone. "Did you send Fran a chain letter as a joke?" he asked Kipp.

Kipp raised an eyebrow. "No."

"You're sure?"

"Yes. What's this about?"

"I'm trying to find out." Tony took his hand off the phone and spoke to Alison again. "Kipp did not send a letter to Fran."

"Could he be pulling your leg?" Alison asked.

Tony glanced at Kipp, who seemed to be worried. Kipp didn't worry easily. "No," Tony said. "Read me the letter."

Alison read it to him all the way through, and with each sentence Tony found himself sinking deeper into the bed. With Neil's first letters it had been the tone that was more disturbing than any specific threats. For they sounded as if they had been written by a brilliant madman, capable of great evil. Even after it had been revealed that Neil was the Caretaker, Tony had never been able to reconcile his friend with writing the letters. They had been so crafty, and Neil had always been so simple. It was almost as if the letters had been dictated to Neil by someone else.

*"I kept wondering and worrying and I tried, but this*

39

*thing got in my head and I couldn't get rid of it. I don't know where it came from. It was like a voice, saying this is true and this is a lie. It wouldn't shut up! I had to listen, and I did listen, and then . . . I did all this."*

"Are you still there?" Alison asked.

"Yes." Tony swallowed. His heart continued to pound—for a different reason now. Yet it was funny —the reasons may have been different, but the anxiety remained the same. It was almost as if his concern over Alison leaving and dating other guys had just culminated in the arrival of the chain letter. In a way he wasn't surprised another one had come.

"There's an ad in the paper," Alison continued. "It's in code like the letter said it would be. It says Fran has to drown her puppy tonight."

Tony had to take a breath. "That's pretty gross."

"Tony, it's got to be a prank. Do you think Joan sent this?"

"I don't know. I'd have to ask her. Have you called her?"

"No. I thought you should. You know her better than I do."

"I don't know her that well."

"I didn't mean anything by it," Alison said.

"I'm sorry."

"Yeah, well, so am I." Alison sighed. "This is the last thing I need in my life right now."

"At least this new Caretaker won't have your address in New York."

"Tony, I'm not even listed at the bottom of the letter. Did I tell you that?"

"No."

"It's interesting, don't you think?"

Tony stopped. When he spoke next, his voice was cold. "Are you suggesting that I sent that letter?"

Alison sounded dismayed. "I don't see how you can think I'd even suggest that. Tony, what's wrong with you? Why are you treating me this way?"

Tony closed his eyes. They were in trouble again, and he had to be cool. Ultimately he was responsible for them being in this situation. After all, he had been the one who had been driving when they hit the man.

"I'm in a bad mood, that's all," he said. "Where was the letter mailed from?"

"Locally."

"Just like before. How's Fran holding up?"

"She's freaking. Who wouldn't? This letter's a lot nastier than the ones Neil sent. It says she's to be horribly killed if she doesn't drown her puppy. What should I tell her?"

"I don't know," he said. "I'll talk to Joan and get back to you. I'll try to get her right now. OK?"

"OK. Call me back even if you don't get her. And Tony?"

"What?"

Alison hesitated. "Nothing."

Tony hung up the phone and related the wording of the letter as best as he could to Kipp. His friend was not amused. He stood and paced the room.

"If Joan didn't send it, then someone outside the group must have got hold of one of Neil's letters," Kipp said.

"Is that possible?" Tony said. "His house burned down. He burned it down with the man's body in it. You remember how he tried to make it look like he had died in the fire? Then, Neil didn't have any letters on him when he died later. I was with him."

"Did we destroy all the letters Neil sent us?" Kipp asked.

"Yeah, I'm sure we did."

"It doesn't really matter. Any one of us could have reconstructed those letters from memory." Kipp thought some more. "Call Joan right now."

Tony dialed her number. He knew it from memory. He had actually been closer to Joan than Alison realized. He had once come within a finger's inch of having sex with her. Sometimes, when things were rough with Alison, he fantasized about calling Joan again and continuing their affair. But he never did. Joan was so gorgeously gross, she intimidated him. Plus he would never cheat on Alison.

He got her mother. Joan was completely unavailable, Mrs. Zuchlensky reported. She was backpacking in Yosemite with friends and wouldn't be home for three days. Tony left the message that she should return his call as soon as possible. He set down the phone and turned back to Kipp.

"Joan's up in the mountains," Tony said. "She's unreachable until Thursday."

"That's convenient," Kipp said.

"Yes and no. If Joan was pulling a prank like this, she would have to stay around. Her absence would cast suspicion on her."

"That's true," Kipp said. "Is it possible Fran and Brenda and Alison are playing a prank on us?"

Tony remembered the fear in Alison's voice. "I somehow doubt it."

"But Alison is mad at you."

Tony shook his head. "This isn't her style."

Kipp walked over to his window and stared out. "Then we might have ourselves a big problem. Another Caretaker—Jesus, who would have thought. Alison's right, this guy sounds a lot nastier than Neil did."

"Do you honestly think Fran's in danger? I've got to call Alison back and tell them something."

Kipp smiled, but it wasn't because he was happy. "I don't think she'll be in danger if she drowns her puppy."

"Kipp! She's not going to do that."

Kipp was sympathetic. "I know. Call them and tell them Joan's in the mountains. Tell them it's probably just her idea of a sick joke."

"Alison won't buy it. This letter was mailed locally."

"How long has Joan been camping?"

"Her mom said a week already," Tony said.

"That's not good." Kipp sat down beside Tony. "Can I ask you a stupid question?"

"Sure."

"Do you want to go to the police with the letter?"

Tony was horrified by the idea. "If we do that, we'll have to explain everything—the whole story will come out. They'll put us in jail."

43

"It was just a suggestion. It would be a crazy thing to do without talking to Joan first. When did you say she'd be back?"

"Thursday."

"When does the next person on the list have to receive the chain letter?"

"Thursday," Tony said.

Kipp laughed. It was his way of coping with the stress, Tony understood. Their situation was totally preposterous. "Then if Fran is still alive on Thursday, we'll have nothing to worry about."

Tony nodded. "She'll be fine."

But his words sounded hollow even to himself. Like when he was trying to tell himself Alison loved him, when he knew in the end she was going to leave him.

# CHAPTER FOUR

When Eric Valence was ten years old, he read all of the Sherlock Holmes books. He walked around in an imaginary world fancying himself Dr. Watson and carrying on intricate conversations with the great detective. In high school he fell in love with Agatha Christie. He read all of her more than eighty murder mysteries word for word, and in over half of them he figured out who the villain was before the master herself revealed the truth.

After graduating from high school, he had his heart set on becoming a hotshot homicide detective. The problem was he'd had serious ear infections as a child, and as a result he was totally deaf in his right ear and had only fifty percent normal hearing in his left. Half a working ear was plenty to keep him from being seriously handicapped. He could enjoy movies and talk comfortably on the phone, as long as the other person spoke directly into the mouthpiece. Unfortunately he couldn't pass the physical to enter the police academy. He had tried three times and had even attempted unsuccessfully to bribe the administering physician. But the men in blue didn't want him, and it was difficult to study by himself to be a competent private eye. He'd planned to become a PI after he had honed his skills on the force. Not that he had given up on his dream. He would be a PI someday. It was just going to take longer than he hoped.

Eric had an uncle who was a cop with the LAPD—Sergeant John Valence. The man was neither a detective nor much of a police officer. He was basically a nice fat guy who had passed a civil service exam when he was twenty-four years old and out of work. Uncle John had driven around in a black-and-white for a few years and eventually found himself where he really belonged, behind a desk pushing papers and talking about all the great crimes other men had solved. Surprisingly, though, the man had done a brief stint with the homicide department, and the stories he could tell were wonderful. All the bodies and the coroners' reports and the smoking pistols—they made Eric's trigger finger twitch just to listen to the man.

But even better than all the talk was the fact that in his position as desk sergeant at the West Covina branch of the LAPD Eric's uncle had access to the computers where the files of literally hundreds of unsolved murders were stored. In a weak moment Eric's uncle had given him the secret codes that tapped into the files, a serious sharing of confidences because there existed tons of information in the files that had never been made known to the public. From that moment on, Eric was in heaven. He would drive to the station from night classes at Claremont College —Eric was majoring in computer science, which he felt was the future for detective work—chat with his uncle for a few minutes, then plug himself into a terminal at the back of the station. Some nights Eric stayed at the terminal until the sun came up and the morning crew came on. People had done so many horrible things to each other in L.A. over the past twenty years—it was wonderful.

Eric Valence was on such a late-night vigil with the police computer when he came across the file on the late Neil Hurly. Eric almost skipped over it. The file didn't appear to be that of an unsolved murder case. But a sentence did catch his eye. One from the county coroner. Apparently this Neil—he was only eighteen at the time of his death—had perished in a fire in his home. His body had been so badly burned that identification of his remains had been difficult. The situation had been further complicated by the fact that there were no current dental records available on Neil. In summary, the coroner wrote that an emerald ring on the victim's left hand had been used to substantiate that it was Neil Hurly who had gone up in smoke. The matter was further verified by the mother's testimony that her son had been sleeping alone at home when the fire broke out. In other words, case closed.

The thing that got Eric about the report was that it had been an emerald ring that had gone through the fire. Eric was no expert when it came to jewelry, but it just so happened that the year before he had been seriously involved with a girl named Meryl Runion, who had an expensive appetite for emeralds. Naturally, because he thought he was in love at the time, and because Meryl twisted his arm about the matter, he tried to buy her an emerald ring for her birthday. Being a practical man on a limited budget, however, he did a little research before making his purchase. One of the things he discovered about emeralds was that they did not make good stones to set in rings. They were soft, and they chipped easily. An expensive emerald could be ruined just by forgetting to remove it before washing the dishes. Eric decided that he should buy Meryl an emerald set in a necklace or a bracelet. But then Meryl met this young lawyer who drove a red Porsche and forgot to return his calls. Eric didn't buy her anything.

Eric was instantly suspicious of the identification of Neil Hurly's remains. If Neil Hurly had been wearing an emerald while lying in a burning house, the emerald should have been destroyed. Yet the coroner's note indicated the emerald had survived the fire intact. How many coroners knew of the softness of an emerald? Eric was only familiar with the gem's fragile nature by chance. It made him wonder if the ring had been placed on the body's hand after the fire. If that was so, it raised an even more startling question.

Was it Neil Hurly who had died in the fire?

The file contained X-rays of what was left of Neil's skull and teeth. As stated, the X-rays had done the coroner no good because he had no dental records for comparison. Eric doubted that the man had tried hard to find records. Why should he? The mom was probably right down the hall saying, "That's my son who died, I know it." Eric studied Neil's history. He had moved to Los Angeles from Canyon, Arkansas, at the age of fourteen. Canyon was listed as Neil's place of birth. In all those fourteen years Neil must have gone to the dentist at least once.

Eric sat back from the terminal. He had no idea where Canyon was in Arkansas. It was probably a small town, and that fact should help him. He didn't waste time speculating on the matter. He called Information and got the area code for Arkansas—it had only one. Then he called Information there. Canyon was tiny. All told, the information assistant gave him a list of three dentists, and two of those were a husband and wife team who shared an office. Eric jotted the numbers down on a notepad. He was already opening his own file on Neil Hurly. There was something not quite right—he could sense it. "Something's afoot," as Holmes might have said to Watson.

Eric was not able to call the dentists until morning. He did so from his apartment, identifying himself as an assistant coroner with the LAPD. The lie went over well because he was able to use his uncle as a reference, calling him the officer in charge of the case. Eric had yet to tell his uncle what he was doing, but he doubted that the dentists would check. As it turned out, the couple had no Neil Hurly in their files. But the secretary of the third guy, Dr. Krane, remembered the Hurlys well. She sounded about eighty years old but very bright.

"Of course I knew Neil," she said. "He was such a sweet young man. They moved to Los Angeles when

Neil was about to enter high school. Would it be all right to ask why you need his X-rays?"

It was clear the woman knew nothing about Neil's supposed death. Eric made his voice sound older. "I'm afraid, madam, we have reason to believe that Neil Hurly has been the victim of fire at his house. There are few remains, and we need the X-rays to make a positive identification."

The woman sounded distressed. "That's horrible. Was the mother killed as well?"

Eric didn't want to complicate the matter by having the mother alive. It was always possible Dr. Krane's secretary would want a permission note from the mother before releasing the X-rays.

"I'm afraid she perished in the fire," Eric said, feeling like a jerk.

"That's so sad," the woman replied. "Do you and your fellow experts think it was an accident?"

"The case is still open." Eric cleared his throat. "Could you please mail the X-rays overnight express to the following address? It would be much appreciated."

"Of course." He could hear her reaching for a pen. "I'm ready."

Eric gave her the address of the West Covina police station in care of Sergeant John Valence. Then he got off the phone quickly. His heart was pounding, but he was feeling good.

He walked into the station the next evening beside his uncle. John was surprised when Eric snapped the overnight mail envelope out of his box before he could go through it.

"What are you up to?" his uncle asked with a twinkle in his eye. At the station Christmas party Sergeant Valence was always the first choice to play Santa Claus. There was a jolliness about him that Eric found endearing.

"I'll tell you when I know something exciting," Eric promised.

His uncle shook his head. "Just don't get me in trouble. I have only a year before my pension."

Eric hurried back to the computer and compared the dentist's X-rays to those of the coroner. The coroner's photographs of his X-rays did not have the high-quality resolution of the dentist's X-rays, but it didn't matter. Eric was no specialist, but even he could see at a glance that the X-rays were from two different people. Neil had had a series of fillings on the lower right side of his mouth when he was thirteen. The guy who had burned to death in Neil's house had no fillings on that side.

Neil Hurly had not burned to death in the Hurly home. But someone had wanted it to look as if he had.

Who?

Why?

The questions of an unfolding mystery. Eric was bursting with excitement. This was better than sex with Meryl Runion. Well, he wouldn't know that for sure. They had actually never done it. But it was better than making out with her. Meryl had always had bad breath.

Eric went in search of Mrs. Hurly's new address. He couldn't find it. She wasn't in the phone book. But he did have her old address, the place where the house had burned to the ground. If he went to the neighborhood and asked around, he should be able to find out where she was living. He had already decided that when he got her new address, he'd drop by the house rather than call her. He'd show the woman the evidence and see how she reacted. For all he knew, she might have been the one who set the whole thing up.

Eric briefly wondered if Neil would answer the door.

# CHAPTER FIVE

For the gang Thursday came and left with no drama. Alison spent the day with Fran, going to the mall and the movies. Fran held up surprisingly well, only crying once over dinner. Alison stayed by her side until twelve midnight. It was Alison's plan to stay overnight, but Fran said it wasn't necessary. Her parents were home sleeping, and besides, Fran snored like a bear and was always embarrassed to have anyone else sleep in the same room with her. Alison left her with a hug and a promise to call in the morning.

Alison did call Fran on Friday morning, and her old friend was just fine. The news spread through the group, and Tony and Kipp began to relax. Brenda didn't, however. It was unnecessary, she said. She hadn't been worried initially. Joan had called her mom to tell her she had decided to spend an extra day in the mountains, so she was still unavailable.

Then Friday night arrived.

Alison went to bed early. Tony was still not talking to her, and the stress was wearing her out. She drank a glass of warm milk and crawled under her covers. The last thing she remembered before falling asleep was that Fran had told her she was going downtown that night to some party.

Then Alison was asleep, and she had no more conscious thoughts.

But curious images did float in her unconscious mind, bringing with them strange sensations. She was in a wide open space but felt claustrophobic. The air pulsed in nauseating patterns of red and purple light. A painful throbbing sound seemed to come from every quarter, totally out of sync with the oscillating colors. There was also a haze of smoke that stank of rotten eggs. But most of all was her intense feeling of despair. It wrapped like a steel coil around her heart and brought pain.

As Alison listened in her dream, she thought she could hear the distant wails of people in torment. Their faint cries came to her through the din of the throbbing and were so twisted they could have been the sounds of animals being tortured to death. But she could see no one, even though she herself felt watched. It was as if the horrible space had eyes of its own, made out of the sickening light and deafening noise. Eyes that were constantly aware and always displeased. Above all else, she wished to God she could be anywhere but where she was.

Then suddenly she was sitting bolt upright in bed—in the dark, where all bad things happened. The phone beside her bed was ringing, and her heart shrieked in her chest. She reached over and grabbed it.

"Hello?"

"Alison?"

"Yeah." She had to take a breath. "Who is this?"

"Mrs. Darey."

The fear came in a wash, instantaneously. "Is something wrong with Fran? What's happened to her?"

Mrs. Darey wept. "I don't know. The hospital called. They say she's been in a car accident. They wouldn't say how she was. They want me to come to the hospital, but my husband's not here, and I'm so upset I can't find my glasses. Ali, can you take me to the hospital? I don't think I can drive like this."

Alison realized the woman had momentarily forgotten that she lived almost an hour away in the valley. She spoke gently. "Sure, I can take you to the hospital. But it might take me a while to get to your house. I'm going to have my boyfriend, Tony, come over and get you instead. You've met him. Then I'm going to drive directly to the hospital and meet you there. Would that be OK?"

"I suppose." Sobs poured from the poor woman. "When they won't tell you how your daughter is, does that mean she's dead?"

"No, Mrs. Darey. It only means they're not sure yet what's wrong with her. There might be nothing wrong with Fran. I'm sure there isn't. Now give me the name of the hospital that called you."

Mrs. Darey was able to convey the vital information. Alison reassured her once more and then hung up and called Tony. He answered immediately. He hadn't been asleep—she could tell by his voice. She glanced at the clock. It was one in the morning.

"Tony, it's Alison. Bad news."

"Fran?"

"Yes. Her mom just called. Fran's been in an accident."

"Tell me about it."

Alison gave him what information she had. Tony said he could be at Fran's house in ten minutes. He sounded alert but calm, far from the way she felt. If anything had happened to Fran, she was never going to forgive herself for having let her go out alone.

"You were waiting for this, weren't you?" Alison asked. "You've been staying up."

"I was waiting for something," Tony said. "I didn't know what it would be."

Alison almost choked on the question. "Do you think she's dead?"

Tony sighed. "I try not to think these days. It makes my head hurt."

Fran Darey was dead.

The three of them got the news at the same time. Although Alison had considerably farther to drive to the hospital, it had taken Tony a while to get Mrs. Darey out of her house and into his car. She had been so overcome with grief. Fran's mother fainted when she heard the news. A team of white coats suddenly appeared and wheeled her away on a gurney. Alison's head was spinning. The doctor who had delivered the news to them could have been telling them Fran had a bad cold—from the tone of his voice. He was middle-aged, and his green surgical gown was splashed with dried blood. He worked the emergency room in the center of the city, where shootings and stabbings were a way of life. He probably told people their loved ones were dead all the time. No sweat off his back.

"How did this happen?" Alison moaned to the doctor as she sagged into Tony's strong arms.

The doctor shook his head. "Ask the police. They're out back with the ambulance drivers. I understand she drove straight into a tree."

Alison asked a stupid question. "Are you sure she's dead? I mean, couldn't she somehow be revived if you tried real hard?"

The doctor regarded her with a blank expression. "She's as dead as they come. We won't be able to revive her. I'm sorry."

Tony wanted to check on Mrs. Hurly. He looked shaken but still in control. Alison let him go. She wanted to talk to the police before they disappeared. She caught one of them in the parking lot as he was climbing into his squad car.

"Excuse me," she said. "I'm a friend of that girl who was just brought in. The one in the car crash. Were you at the scene of the accident?"

The officer was young and handsome. He had a neat brown mustache and a dark blue uniform that fit him perfectly. He stood outside his car with her. His face supplied the sympathy the doctor's had been missing.

"Yes, I was, miss," he said and touched her arm. "I'm very sorry your friend was killed. I understand she was only eighteen."

Alison nodded and sniffed. "I'm sorry, too. But I'm also confused. The doctor inside said Fran ran straight into a tree?"

"That's correct. The tree was a tall olive at the side of the road. She must have been doing sixty when she hit it. Both the tree and the car were destroyed."

"Do you think she was run off the road?"

"There was no sign of skid marks. Usually when someone runs you off the road, you have a chance to hit the brakes. But maybe not. The accident's going to be thoroughly investigated. I wish I could tell you more. I really am sorry."

Alison started to turn away and go back inside to find Tony. She needed his strong arms now more than ever. She just hoped that when she found him, he would open his arms to her. Yet she hesitated before leaving and asked the officer what was probably another stupid question. It was just something she felt she had to ask.

"How exactly did Fran die?" she asked.

The police officer looked uncomfortable. "From the force of the impact."

"Her body got smashed between the car and the tree?"

The cop fidgeted. "Not exactly, but close enough. I can tell you for certain that she died instantly."

The odd purple color of the chain letter envelope flashed in her mind, along with the sick purple and red lights of the nightmare she'd been having when the phone rang. She remembered the dream then—the invisible people crying in the smoky distance. It was a memory that made her shudder.

"Tell me exactly how it was," she said.

The officer looked down. "You don't want to know."

58

"I need to know."

"Her head went through the windshield and struck a thick branch of the tree at an unfavorable angle. That broke her neck and—"

"And what?"

The officer looked puzzled. "I've been to a hundred serious car accidents, and I don't know how it happened. It must have been the shattered glass of the windshield in combination with the impact of her skull on the tree."

"What are you saying?"

The officer lowered his gaze once more. "Your friend was decapitated in the accident. We found her head in a nearby bush."

# CHAPTER SIX

$S$aturday morning the surviving members of the original ill-fated "gang" met at the city park beside a kiddie rocket ship in the play area. Joan Zuchlensky was present, finally back from hiking in the mountains. The gang had met in the same spot a few months earlier, after Kipp received notice of his "small service" to perform. That time Kipp only had to tell everybody he cheated on his SATs to please the Caretaker. But life had become tougher. Kipp received a letter in the mail that morning, even though Fran hadn't passed hers on to him. Fran's name was no longer on the list, but otherwise the letter was identical to the one Fran had received. A coded ad had appeared in that morning's edition of the *Times*. Decoded it said:

Burn sister's entire right arm.

"Who wants to open this meeting?" Alison asked. She was sitting on the park bench outside the concrete circle that surrounded the rocket ship and the playing sand, Brenda beside her. Of them all, Tony decided,

Alison looked the palest. Of course, she had been the closest to Fran. Yet none of them looked too hot. Even Kipp had lost his smile. He was very protective of his little sister.

"We don't need to formally open it," Joan said. "We just need to start talking."

"Fine," Alison said. "We'll all start talking at once."

"Are you going to hassle me?" Joan asked Alison. "Because if you are, I'd just as soon leave now."

Alison seemed to be too hurt to argue. "I'm not going to hassle you."

"Good," Joan replied. She wasn't dressed in her usual leather and metal style. Her platinum hair was short and unadorned, almost as white as her T-shirt. She had on blue jeans, a shade too much lipstick, but a pound less makeup than when she was in school. Her voice sounded tough as ever, though.

"Why don't I start things off," Kipp said, sitting at the end of the rocket slide with the chain letter in his lap. "I'll list what we know about this letter and the situation as a whole. Then I'll list what we don't know."

"Sounds good," Tony mumbled. He was sitting in the sand, off to the side from everyone else. It was eleven in the morning, and he hadn't gone to bed yet. Maybe when the others left, he would lie down in the sand and take a nap.

"This new chain letter was written by someone who knew about Neil's chain letters," Kipp began. "The wording is almost identical. The envelope it came in *is* identical. But this chain letter can't have come from

61

Neil because he's dead. That's a fact. Tony buried him. But the person who wrote this new letter also knows how far Neil took us through his 'Columns.' You'll remember we were all in Column Two when the truth finally came out. This person has started us off in Column Three. You all follow where this is leading?"

"Neil had an accomplice," Alison said.

"It seems like it," Kipp said. "And a mean one at that."

"Neil didn't have an accomplice," Tony said. "He was my friend. I was with him when he died. He would have told me."

"He didn't tell you he was the Caretaker to begin with," Brenda said.

Tony shook his head. "It's not possible."

"I have to agree with Brenda," Kipp said carefully. "Neil was physically and mentally ill. He was very weak toward the end. Having an accomplice would explain how he was able to do all the stuff he did before he died."

"If Neil had an accomplice," Tony asked, "how come this person didn't know about Alison? She's not on the list."

"I can't explain that," Kipp admitted.

"Wait a second," Joan interrupted. "We're acting like babies. How do we know this new Caretaker was responsible for Fran's death? She ran into a tree. The police think it was an accident."

"It could have been an accident," Tony said. "We all know how upset she was. She couldn't have been driving very well."

"I suppose it's possible," Kipp said. "But it's a hell of a coincidence."

"Are you guys nuts?" Alison broke in. "The Caretaker promised Fran would die if she didn't drown her puppy. Well, she didn't and she's dead. That's not coincidence. That's cause and effect. And are you forgetting how she died? She was decapitated! Talk about a horrible death." Tears sprang into Alison's eyes. "Let's not fool ourselves that she wasn't murdered."

"I think you're being overly dramatic," Joan told Alison. "People lose their heads in accidents all the time. My dad's a cop, you know. He's told me plenty of stories like this."

"The cop who was at the scene of the accident didn't know how it could have happened," Alison said bitterly.

"He was probably a rookie," Joan said.

"Goddamn you, I talked to him!" Alison swore.

"Hold on, you two," Kipp interrupted. "Both of you are making good points. As I said, that Fran should suddenly die is an amazing coincidence. But if she was murdered by the new Caretaker, how did he do it? Fran was in a devastating car crash. The Caretaker couldn't have been in the car with her when she crashed. He wouldn't have survived. That leaves the possibility that she was run off the road. But even the cop Alison talked to didn't think that was likely."

"He didn't say it was impossible, though," Alison muttered.

"All right," Kipp said. "Let's say she was run off the road. What about her losing her head?"

"Would you guys please quit hammering that point?" Brenda asked, and now she began to get teary as well. "You're making me sick."

"We have to talk about it," Kipp said. "We have to talk about everything that's happened if we're to get out of this situation alive. Now, how was she decapitated if not by the accident alone? Did the person who ran her off the road stop and hack off her head?"

"It's possible," Alison said.

"Not really," Kipp said. "The guy would have had a few minutes at best. It's hard to cut someone's head off. You'd need a saw, and a coroner would spot saw marks immediately. It must have been the impact with the tree in combination with the shattered windshield—like the cop told you, Alison."

Alison stared at him. "I cannot believe that you of all people, Kipp, could turn this into a simple accident."

"I'm not," Kipp replied. "I believe she could have been run off the road. I'm simply not buying the scenario that she was purposely decapitated."

"Could we move on, please?" Brenda complained.

"We have to come to conclusions before we move on," Kipp said. "Was Fran's death an accident or not? Let's take a vote."

"I say it was an accident," Joan said.

Brenda glanced at Alison. "Accident," Brenda said.

"Brenda!" Alison said in disbelief.

"It doesn't make sense she could have been murdered while driving down the street in her own car," Brenda said. She gave Alison a quick hug. "I'm sorry."

"It was no accident," Alison insisted, pushing Brenda away.

"What do you think, Tony?" Kipp asked.

The question startled Tony. He had been watching and listening but from a distance. He had almost forgotten that he was part of the group. It might have been the stress of Fran's death and the missed night of sleep, but his old friends all looked like strangers to him. These people he had gone to school with for years. Even Alison. They had hardly spoken to each other before they parted at the hospital the night before.

"I think we're not seeing the big picture," Tony said. "I think we're asking ourselves the wrong questions."

"Whether Fran's death was accidental or not is a vital question," Kipp said.

"Do you think it was an accident?" Tony asked him.

"I just don't know," Kipp said. "Do you?"

Tony shrugged. "Who knows? Who can know? Something weird is going on, that's for sure."

Kipp showed impatience. "What's your point?"

"Who's sending these chain letters and why?" Tony asked. "That's the only thing that matters. All this other stuff is just that—stuff."

"I agree," Joan said.

"All right," Kipp said. "We can talk about that. Do you have any suggestions, Tony?"

Tony nodded. "The loose end we had last time, after we found out the Caretaker was Neil, was that we never discovered who the dead man in the desert was."

65

"Do you think someone connected to him might be sending the letters?" Alison asked.

"Yes," Tony said.

"Why?" Alison asked.

"Revenge," Tony said. "We ran the guy over, after all."

"We don't know that for sure," Kipp said quickly. "Talking about him won't do us any good. We talked about him three months ago and went around in circles. We don't know who the man was, and we're probably never going to know who he was. We've got to take steps that can help us right now——"

"Last time it was one of us," Joan interrupted, eyeing Alison. "It could be one of us again."

"None of us would kill Fran," Alison said.

"She was scared," Joan said. "She ran off the road."

"Yeah, while you were conveniently unavailable," Alison snapped at her. Joan jumped up, fire in her eyes.

"Are you saying I wrote these sick letters?" Joan demanded.

"You're the only one in the group who's sick enough to have done it," Alison shouted back, and the fact that she was contradicting herself of a moment ago didn't seem to bother her.

"You bitch," Joan swore, taking a dangerous step toward Alison.

Alison stood slowly. "What are you going to do, Joany? Try to make my day?"

"Stop it," Tony said quietly. "Joan is not the Caretaker."

Alison gazed at him incredulously. "I can't believe you're taking her side."

Joan laughed. "Looks like you don't have him wrapped around your little finger like you thought."

Tony waved away both of them. "You two fight whenever you get together. Sit down and let's figure out what we have to do next."

Alison continued to stare at him before she nodded. "All right," she said and sat back down. Joan strolled over and leaned against the rocket ship, studying her nails and looking bored. Kipp resumed command of the group.

"The demands made in these new letters are much stronger than Neil's ever were," Kipp said. "In fact, if they continue the way they're going, none of us is going to do any of them. I'm sure as hell not going to hurt Leslie."

"But what if it's a choice between hurting her and being killed?" Brenda asked Kipp, real anxiety in her voice. Kipp's reaction was a combination of fondness and surprise.

"But you said you thought what happened to Fran was an accident," he said.

"Kipp, I'm serious," Brenda said. "What if?"

Kipp was disgusted. "There is no *what if*. I'm not going to burn my sister's arm. It's as simple as that."

"Why don't we go to the police?" Alison suddenly blurted out.

Tony sat up with a start. "Are you kidding?"

"No, I'm not kidding," Alison said firmly. "With everything that happened with Neil, no one died.

No one was even hurt, except Neil. But this round of letters has only begun, and already one of us is dead. We can't fool around this time. We have to go to the police."

"If we go to the police, I go to jail," Tony said flatly. "If that's what the rest of you want, tell me now. I'll have to find myself a lawyer."

"You don't have to go to jail," Alison said.

Tony felt a stab of anger. "You know what I love? I love it that out of everyone in this group, you're the one who's making this suggestion. I just love it, Ali."

His words pierced her like a sword. She shook her head slightly and stared at him some more, but now there were more tears to cloud her vision. He didn't care, he told himself. He couldn't believe that his welfare wasn't a prime consideration of hers.

"Tony probably would go to jail if we went to the police," Kipp said. "He was the one who was driving when we hit the man."

"But it was Joan who punched out the car lights on him," Brenda broke in. "If it weren't for her, Tony wouldn't have hit anybody."

"If it weren't for your beer, I wouldn't have been so drunk that I wanted to punch out the lights!" Joan yelled.

"Stop it!" Kipp raised his hand. "We're all involved in this. All of us helped bury the man. None of us reported what happened to the police. We could all go to jail. I was just pointing out that Tony is in the most vulnerable position."

"Yeah," Joan said to Alison. "You don't care what

happens to your boyfriend. You're just interested in saving your own skin."

Alison closed her eyes and took a deep breath. Tears trickled over her cheeks. As angry as he was, Tony had to restrain himself from getting up and wiping her tears away. He hated to see Alison cry. Of course he cared. And maybe she was right. Maybe it was time to go to the police. But it was a suggestion he was not going to second. There had to be a better way out of this madness. They just had to find it. Alison reopened her eyes and scanned everyone.

"I'll go along with what the group decides," she said. "I'm not trying to hurt anybody, least of all Tony. But I want Kipp to go away for the next few days. I want him to disappear to a place none of us have heard of."

"I think that's a good idea," Brenda said, nodding in the direction of her boyfriend. "You're getting out of here, Kipp."

"I can't go now," Kipp said. "I'm leaving for MIT soon. I have things to do."

Brenda got up. She walked over and slapped Kipp on the head. "You're not going to argue with me!" she shouted. "You're going to leave today because you're not going to die."

"All right, I'll go," Kipp said, trying to protect himself from another blow with a raised arm.

"When my turn comes, I'll split," Joan said. "It'll be better than running off and crying to the police."

Tony got up and wiped the sand off his butt. "Are we done? Have we decided to do nothing? If that's it, I've got to go."

Alison also stood. "Do you have any other suggestions about what we should do, Tony?" she asked.

He eyed her across the distance between them. It wasn't far—maybe fifteen feet. But she could have been on the far side of the moon as far as he was concerned. He felt no contact, no connection, between them. It made him more sad than angry. They were under attack, and from the outside. A common enemy usually brought people together, but that wasn't the case here. Maybe they'd been too quick to dismiss the possibility that the Caretaker was one of them. Tony's heart was aching so badly, it was as if the attack were coming from within.

"I have nothing else to say," Tony replied. He turned and walked away.

# CHAPTER SEVEN

It was good to come home to the old school. It was only across the street from the park, and Tony walked there without going back for his car. He climbed the fence that enclosed the football stadium and track. Ah, the stadium—the site of his adolescent glory. It was good to see it, but at the same time it filled him with revulsion. All the things he had done in high school to construct an invincible self-image. Of what use was that image to him now? He was tired and his back ached and he had an unseen monster on his tail. He wished his name were at the top of the list instead of Kipp's. It would be good to see what his task was and get it over. It might be even better to refuse the task and meet the monster head-on. Sometimes he imagined he saw the new Caretaker when he looked in the mirror.

Tony walked out onto the field, marveling at the silence. He couldn't remember a time when he had played football or run track with the stands completely empty. What a shallow jerk he'd been. He'd always needed an audience in order to perform.

A sudden desire to run came to him right then. He had shorts and running shoes on. Even though his spine hurt, his doctor had said light jogging shouldn't aggravate his condition. He'd been a good runner once—a great one, in fact. He'd won league championships in the quarter mile and the half mile. Some of that old endurance must still be with him.

Tony walked back out to the track and began to run around the cinder oval. His pace was slow at first, but it wasn't long before he found his rhythm and began to pick up speed. Soon he had his stride stretched almost to full. He was breathing hard, but it didn't feel hard. It was a release for him—driving his body forward, around and around the track. The exercise was like a penance—for all the real and imagined crimes he had committed. He ran a mile, then two, three. He ran over four miles, and by the time he stopped, every muscle in his body was limp. He staggered into the center of the field and plopped down flat on his back in the grass beneath the warm, clear sky. He didn't remember closing his eyes. His last conscious thought was of wanting to float up into the heavens, to leave the world behind.

Then he was asleep.

In his dream he was floating in an alien sky.

The space was not blue, but red and purple, filled with heavy pounding sounds and thick smoke that stank of sulfur. In this abyss of unpleasantness he floated like a drifting balloon, fearful of passing too close to a hidden flame. It wasn't as though the place was hot. It was simply that the threat of painful fire existed, just as the place existed. But perhaps it was the faint cries he heard in the distance that invoked his fear. They didn't sound like human cries, or rather, they sounded like cries of creatures that might have once been human but had now become twisted and evil. He didn't know how this sense came to him. It was just there, as he was there, without explanation. The consciousness brought no relief. It only deepened his horror.

His drifting continued. Yet he began to feel that there was a destination to his course. He sensed rather than saw the great wall that lay before him. He knew it was a wall to separate him from where he was and where he could end up—if he made the wrong choice. But as horrible as the space was in which he was floating, he knew that beyond the wall there existed true despair. For it was from there that the cries emanated. The cries that prayed only for a death that would lead to nonexistence.

Yes, there was definitely a wall ahead. He could see it now. It was dark, but not so thick that he couldn't catch a sense of what was on the far side. . . .

Tony awoke to find a sky the color of twilight above him. At first he couldn't believe he'd slept away the entire day. But then he sat up and looked around and the evidence of his eyes couldn't be denied. It was no wonder, actually. It had been so long since he'd rested.

Tony got up and walked to the fence that enclosed the stadium. He had trouble scaling the wire mesh—his limbs felt oddly disconnected from his torso. It took him half an hour to walk back to his car on the far side of the park, although the car was less than a mile from where he had slept. By the time he got behind his steering wheel, his legs were cold and he had a headache. He had been getting so many headaches lately that he kept a bottle of Tylenol on his dashboard. He took out a couple of tablets and chewed them slowly without water. They left a bitter taste in his mouth. He remembered then that he'd had a nightmare while lying in the center of the football field. But no details of it came to him.

Tony was putting the bottle of Tylenol back onto the dashboard when he noticed the scrap of paper sitting there. He picked it up and studied it in the stark halogen light from a nearby street lamp. It was Sasha's phone number. He smiled at the memory of her, and the smile felt like a welcome stranger on his face. She had told him to call him some night when he needed a massage. What was wrong with right then? He checked his watch. It was only seven o'clock. He needed someone to talk to, other than the people in the group. Certainly he didn't feel like talking to Alison. He couldn't get over how she had wanted to hand him over to the police, even before they were certain Fran's death was anything more than an accident. Alison had a thing or two to learn about devotion.

Tony drove to a nearby phone booth and dialed Sasha's number. He didn't really expect to catch her in. It was, after all, Saturday night. She was an attractive young lady, and she probably had a line of men waiting outside her door.

She answered on the third ring.

"Hello?"

"Hi, Sasha? This is Tony. I met you at the mall the other day. Do you remember me?"

She took a moment, then said, "Tony, yeah, sure I remember you. How are you doing?"

"I'm all right. How are you?"

Her voice was warm and easy. "Fine. A little bored. What are you up to?"

"Nothing. Actually, I was wondering if you were doing anything?"

"No. Why? Did you want to stop by?"

"Not if it would be inconvenient."

"It's no problem. Come over. Maybe we can go out and have a drink together."

"That sounds like fun." Tony worried if he'd be able to get into a bar. He'd never been in one before. "Where do you live?"

Sasha gave him her address. It wasn't far from where he was. He said goodbye and hung up. He found himself smiling again. The thought of Alison tried to enter his mind, but he pushed it away.

Sasha lived in a new apartment complex not far from the mall where they had met. She greeted him at her door wearing black pants and a white blouse. Her maroon hair hung long down her back. Her green eyes shone as she looked at him, and her lips were a wonderful red around a friendly smile. Fortunately he'd had an extra shirt and pair of pants in his car that he'd changed into. The shorts he'd run in were still soaked with sweat. Sasha invited him in.

"Forgive the mess," she said as she strode from the living room into the kitchen. The apartment was

75

small but neat. The only mess was a couple of paperbacks and a half-filled mug sitting on a coffee table. The furniture seemed to be of high quality. Tony briefly wondered if her family lived in the area, and if they helped her out. He wasn't entirely sure what her job at the hospital was. She seemed a tad young to be a nurse.

The apartment had a faint medicinal smell to it—not alcohol, something else. He asked her about it as he sat at her kitchen table. She had made coffee and wanted him to have a cup before they went out. The question seemed to embarrass her.

"Is it noticeable?" she asked.

He wished he hadn't asked. "It's not bad."

She forced a laugh. "To tell you the truth, I think it's me. The smell of the clinic gets on my clothes and in my hair. I can't get it out. The only time I don't smell is right after I've taken a shower." She glanced over at him. "When I'm naked."

Tony grinned. "I guess I caught you at a bad time, then."

Sasha brought him a mug of steaming coffee. "It's a good time. Do you take it black or with cream?"

"I like a little milk and sugar in it, thank you."

Sasha turned back to the refrigerator. "I like it scalding hot and black. I like to feel it burn my insides as it goes down. Pretty weird, huh? All the girls at work drink it the same way."

"What exactly do you do at the hospital?" Tony asked.

"As little as possible." She brought him milk and

sugar. "I'm thinking of quitting my job and leaving the area."

"Oh, that's too bad."

She sat across from him and regarded him with her big green eyes. "Why?" she asked seriously.

He shrugged. "I just met you is all. You seem like an interesting person."

She liked that answer. "How did you like the way I asked you out at the mall?"

"Did you ask me out?"

"I did and you know it." She regarded him closely, in an oddly penetrating way that made him nervous. "But I could tell you liked me. I knew you'd call."

Tony blushed. "Does this mean I don't get a massage?"

Sasha blushed as well and was even more beautiful. For the blood gave color to her face, which was quite pale.

"You can have a massage and then some, Tony," she said.

They didn't go to a bar but to a nightclub that played music at several decibels above the comfort level. The lighting was a trip—brilliant strobes that were sequenced with the guitars and vocals. Tony had never been to such a place before and found it exciting. Sasha could really dance—he could hardly keep up with her. Her endurance was extraordinary. They danced fifteen songs in a row before taking a break. She ordered drinks for them while he ran off to the bathroom, and she paid for them. Maybe she did know he was under twenty-one and didn't want to embarrass him by asking. They each had a margarita and a screwdriver—heavy on the lethal fluids. Sasha downed her drinks and ordered another couple while he nursed his first one. He paid for this round, and no one asked any questions. Sasha lit up a cigarette and blew a cloud of smoke in his face. He was surprised a nurse would smoke.

"Are you having fun?" she asked. It was hard to hear her over the music.

"I'm having a great time," he called back.

She continued to peer at him, holding the fire of the cigarette close to her hair. "Something's on your mind," she said.

"No," he said. "I'm fine. I'm glad I'm here with you."

She nodded. "I want you to tell me about it later."

Tony didn't reply, not directly to her remark, and soon they were back out on the dance floor, and it was all he could do to hold himself upright. He had run too far that morning. He had run too fast. He felt as if he'd been on a treadmill for the last three months, and he wondered if this was his first chance to get off. He really liked Sasha. The whole time he was with her, he hardly thought of Alison, and that was a big relief. He could handle the new Caretaker, he thought, if he could just get his heart free of the pain he'd been feeling.

On the way home he was tired and drunk. For safety's sake it would have been better if Sasha had driven. She had drunk twice what he had, but her system seemed to be able to handle it. But it was a masculine thing with him that he had to be the one to drive his car. It was close to midnight. On a long stretch of freeway Sasha again asked him what was on his mind.

"How can you tell something's bothering me?" he asked. He had to concentrate on the road. The red taillights of the cars in front of him kept blurring into bloated sunspots.

"I can see it in your face," she said simply.

He glanced over at her. Her mood was more serious than earlier, but still easy. She had a definite presence. When she asked something, it was hard to resist answering her truthfully.

"What do you see?" he asked.

"You're grieving over another girl."

Tony was shocked. "Huh?"

"What's her name?"

Tony stared straight ahead. "Alison Parker."

Sasha reached over and touched his leg. "You can talk about it. I don't mind."

"There's nothing to say." The car suddenly felt cramped. Yet the touch of her hand on his leg was nice. So nice he was able to lie—a little. "She was a girl I used to date. We broke up."

"You haven't broken up completely." Sasha took her hand back. "Was she unfaithful to you?"

"No. I don't know. I don't think so." He added, "She's leaving the area soon."

Sasha's next question hit him like a slap. "Do you think she's with someone else right now?"

Tony forced a smile. "I hope not."

Sasha leaned closer. He could smell the alcohol on

her breath, but it smelled sweet, not sour. "You're with someone. Why can't she be with someone?"

"She can. I just don't think she is."

Sasha sat back in her seat. "Let's swing by her house on the way to my place. We'll see if she's alone."

He glanced at her, uncertain. "Sasha?"

"It's just a hunch I have, Tony. We'll pay her a visit. Don't worry. She'll never know we were there."

"But I don't want to stop by her house."

"Yes, you do."

# CHAPTER EIGHT

Alison left the park with a heavy heart. She got in her car and drove aimlessly around town. She felt torn apart. She had pain hitting her from all directions. Her friend Fran was dead. They had to bury her on Monday. The murderer was still on the loose, composing fresh letters and tasks for them to complete. Then there was Tony, her beloved Tony, who treated everything she said with distrust and contempt. She couldn't understand where his hatred for her was coming from. She had done nothing to him. She only wanted to live her life to the fullest, with him still a big part of it. Of course, she had suggested they go to the police. It was the only rational thing to do. This Caretaker was not picking at their weak spots. He was going for the jugular, and he liked the taste of blood.

Eventually Alison found herself heading for her house, more than thirty miles from the neighborhood where her friends lived. But when she reached her usual off-ramp, she kept driving. She couldn't face her parents the way she felt. She needed to get away, to get out of the city. She stayed on the freeway, and when the turnoffs came for the mountain resorts, she took one. The ground rose in front of her, and the air cooled. She saw a pine, then half a dozen. The forest thickened steadily the higher she went. Soon she was driving through mountains of green.

She finally realized she was heading toward Big Bear Lake. She didn't want to go there. It was a weekend, and the lake would be crowded. She spotted a sign pointing toward a Green Valley Lake. That sounded nice. She turned left off the main road. Five miles later she caught sight of a crystal-clear body of water. The valley was heavenly and appeared almost deserted. She parked and walked along the water. For the first time all day the lump in her throat began to shrink. There wasn't a cloud in the sky. She took a deep breath and picked up a stone and skimmed it over the glassy water. Five hops—she hadn't lost her touch.

She wasn't the only one skimming rocks on the lake. At the far end of the lake she could just make out a young man in blue jeans and a yellow shirt dancing his pebbles over the surface, too. He didn't throw his rocks hard, but they went forever over the water. *He* had the touch. He noticed her watching him and waved to her. He seemed to be harmless, about her age, with a slight build and light brown hair that was in desperate need of a trim. He smiled as she approached, and a powerful sensation of déjà vu swept over her. Yet she had never been to this lake before. Certainly she couldn't have met this guy before. She was sure of that—well, pretty sure.

"Hi," he said.

"Hello," she replied. She nodded to the rocks in his hands. "How do you get your stones to skip like that? I counted fifteen hops on your last throw."

The sunlight shone in his hair and on his shy expression. "It's all in the wrist." He demonstrated for her, and the rock took close to twenty hops before sinking below the surface. Once more she was struck by the ease with which he threw them. "See, there's nothing to it," he said.

"For you maybe." She looked around. They weren't far from a grass meadow alive with blooming flowers in every color. At the far end of the meadow was a small wooden cabin. It, too, looked familiar to her, but not exactly. It was as if it had been thoroughly described to her, not a place she had ever visited. "Is that your cabin?" she asked, pointing.

"Sometimes I stay there," he said, watching her. "You look tired. Would you like a cup of tea?"

His suggestion was a little forward, but somehow, coming from him, it didn't seem rude. There was something disarming about the guy. Not for a second did she feel in danger. Quite the reverse—it was very pleasant to stand beside him in the warm sunlight among the trees.

"I'm just out for a walk." She chuckled. "I couldn't drop in on you. I mean, I don't even know you."

He let his rocks fall to the ground and offered his hand. "My name's Chris."

She shook his hand. "I'm Alison."

"Ali?"

She smiled. "My friends call me that."

"Ali," he repeated to himself, and it seemed as if he liked the sound of her name. He turned in the direction of his cabin. "Well, I'm going to have tea. You can join me if you wish."

She didn't want him to be gone suddenly. "I think I will," she said.

The inside of his cabin was sparsely furnished. He put an old black kettle on a wood stove. He lit a fire with a match scraped along the wall of the stove. "It'll take a few minutes," he said and stepped back outside onto the front porch, where there were a couple of chairs. He sat down and put his legs up on the railing. After a moment's hesitation, Alison sat beside him. He scanned the nearby lake and sighed with pleasure.

"A day like this makes it hard to leave here," he said.

"Do you have to leave? Do you have to get back to work?" She believed she had miscalculated his age. He didn't look much older than she was, but he had an air about him that spoke of greater maturity.

"I'm only back here for a short time, Ali," he said.

"Where are you from?"

The question amused him. He glanced back at the water. "Not so far from here—if you know how to fly."

She laughed. "So you're Peter Pan?"

He laughed softly, nodding. "If you like."

"What kind of work do you do?"

He thought for a moment. "I'm a farmer."

"Really? What do you grow?"

"Seeds."

"No. Seriously?"

"I grow them, and then I harvest them when the time is right."

She couldn't tell if he was kidding or not. She didn't mind if he was. His whole air was so sweet. He was quite enchanting. He brushed a lock of his brown hair aside and stared at her once more. He was waiting for her to speak.

"Where is your farm?" she asked.

"Near here."

"In the woods?"

"In Los Angeles," he said.

She laughed again. "I'd like to see it, in the middle of the city. What do you grow? People?"

He continued to watch her. "Yes. You have grown up, Ali."

She stopped, confused. "What do you mean?"

"What I said. You are growing up swiftly. That's why you suffer so much. Sometimes the faster you run, the more you trip and hurt yourself. But the sooner you'll reach your goal."

Now she was totally lost. "How do you know anything about me? I've never met you before. Have I?"

"Yes."

"When?"

"Not long ago. Don't worry. You won't remember me."

Alison leaned back in her seat and felt her breath slowly go out of her body. It was true—she had no memory of this guy. Yet she *knew* him. She didn't understand how both things could be true at the same time.

"What am I suffering from now?" she asked carefully.

"Lack of love. It's always the cause of suffering."

She thought of Tony and their unfulfilled love, and her heart ached. "That's true," she whispered. Then she shook herself. "Who are you?"

He removed his legs from the porch rail and sat up. "I'm a guide. I'm here to guide you."

"To what?"

"You know what."

She bit her lower lip, but she didn't taste blood. She tasted cold water. Her whole body had suddenly gone cold. "You know about the chain letters?" she gasped.

He shrugged. "The letters are not important. It's what they represent."

"And what's that?"

"A chain," he said seriously. "An unbroken chain. It's very ancient—not a happy thing. But it can be broken."

Alison's head was spinning. She had come to this spot by chance. She had only met this guy by chance. Yet he knew of her worst fears. . . .

"How can we break it?" she asked.

"With love," he said simply.

"I don't understand."

The guy's green eyes were penetrating, yet gentle still. It was as if she stood fully exposed before him, her thoughts and everything, but it was OK because he understood her. And appreciated her. That's why

she felt so comfortable with him. He radiated uncon-
ditional love.

"You do understand, Ali," he said.

"But I love Tony. I want to help him. I want to help
the others, but they won't listen to me. Tony won't
even talk to me."

The guy raised a finger. "That doesn't matter,
either. You have asked for help, and someone will
come. Trust this person. But beyond this you must
trust what's in your heart. The letters come from a
place where there is no heart. There is only pain.
None of you must go to that place."

Alison was frightened. "Where is that place?"

The guy hesitated. Alison didn't understand why
she didn't think of him as Chris. Then she realized it
was probably because it wasn't his real name. It was
just something he made up so she could understand.
But understand what? Who the hell was this guy?

"It is not far from here, either," he said.

"But this Caretaker has already killed one of us,"
she said. "How can I stop him from killing more of
us?"

"Dying is not so bad as being put in the box."

"What happens when you're put in the box?" Her
voice trembled. "Do you go to that place?"

"Eventually. Unless you can get out. But it's difficult to get out once you are inside. Most people never
do." The kettle began to whistle inside the cabin. The
guy seemed to listen to it for a few moments. Yet
he could have been listening to something far off. His
gaze focused on a place she couldn't see. He came

back to her after a minute, though. "I'm afraid you won't have time to stay for tea," he said, and there was a hint of sorrow in his voice.

"Why not?"

"It is time."

"Time for what?" She stood. "Please, you have to tell me what's happening here. Who are you?"

He stood, too. He didn't say anything but only hugged her, and his arms as they went around her were of great comfort. She felt a warm glow in her chest that spread through her after he let go. But her heart was still in anguish.

"I am your friend," he said. He reached out and touched the hair that hung beside her cheek. "I am your greatest admirer."

"But I don't understand."

"You will. You will act in love. You will do what has to be done."

She began to cry. "I'm afraid. Can't I stay with you a few more minutes?"

He shook his head and turned for the front door. "You have to hurry. Go to where it all began. There are two places, you know. Find them and you will reach the end of the chain." He smiled at her one last time before stepping inside. "Goodbye, Ali."

"But—?"

"Hurry," he said and vanished through the door.

Alison stood for a minute staring at the closed door before opening it and peeking inside. He must have gone out the back way. She saw no sign of him. The whistle of the kettle had stopped. It sat on the wood stove as if it had sat there undisturbed for years. There was no sign of the burning logs. It was as if she had dreamed the entire encounter. She turned and walked back to the lake, toward her car. His words rang true, whoever he was. She had to hurry, even if she didn't know where she was going.

# CHAPTER NINE

Alison was on the main freeway toward her house when she deciphered the mystery the strange fellow had set before her. He had spoken of two places where it had all begun. Obviously the first must be the dusty road in the desert, where they had run over the man. The second had eluded her at first. Neil had started the chain letters. Therefore, the inside of Neil's head must be the second starting point. But Neil was dead. His mind was gone. Yet, she reasoned, he must have sat at home when he composed the chain letters. She would go there, to what was left of the place. She remembered he had burned it down with the man's dead body inside to give the illusion that it was he, Neil, who had been killed by the Caretaker. She didn't want to go to the man's first grave in the desert. She wasn't even sure that she could find it—or what she'd do out in the middle of the desert.

The burned house had months ago been leveled by bulldozers. A grass lot stood in its place. There was plenty of ash left, however. As Alison crept up to the lot in her car, she imagined she was looking at the remains of a bomb blast site—one that had hastily been covered over with sod. She parked and walked across the grass, charred splinters poking at her shoes from between the soft blades. All right, she was here. Now what? Should she sit down cross-legged in the grass and commune with Neil's ghost for answers? She decided she had already met one ghost that day.

*Who was that guy? How did he know about the letters?*

She wasn't going to answer those questions here. She must have misunderstood the guy's clues. She was returning to her car when she saw a new guy climb out of a car. He had just pulled up. The sun was close to setting, and it was hard to see in the dim light. For a moment she was afraid. What could he want here? It was a vacant lot, after all. She was the only thing there.

"Hello?" he called.

"Yeah, what can I do for you?" she asked nervously.

"What?"

"I said, what do you want?"

He walked closer. "My name's Eric Valence. I'm a police officer."

"You don't look like a police officer. Show me your badge."

He stopped in midstride. "I'm off duty."

"Yeah, right. You look like you're off duty from high school." Actually, he didn't look bad for a complete stranger. He was slender, but had broad shoulders and a graceful stance. His features were dark, sharp. He looked intelligent, and she wondered if she should be trying to make a fool out of him without first knowing who he was and what he wanted.

"I'm twenty-one years old," he said.

"Isn't that kind of young to be a police officer?"

"What?"

"Can't you hear?"

He tilted the left side of her head his way. "I can hear," he said, insulted.

*Yeah, but not too well. God, I'm ridiculing someone's handicap.*

She took a step closer to him and spoke louder. "Are you really a police officer? Please tell me the truth."

He hesitated. "I work for the police. My uncle's a sergeant with the LAPD."

"And you just help out every now and then?"

"I'm collecting information for them for a case."

Alison remembered where she was and began to feel nervous. "What kind of case?" she asked.

"I can't go into detail. But I need to find the woman who used to live in this house before it burned down. I've been out to this neighborhood before, but nobody around here seems to know where she's moved to. Do you know who I'm talking about?"

Alison's throat tightened. The police might be on to them already. She had told the group that morning that she wanted to go to the authorities, but it was quite another thing to have the authorities come to them. They'd get no extra credit for turning themselves in.

"I might," she said evasively. "Who are we talking about?"

"Mrs. Katherine Hurly. Do you know her?"

She shrugged. "A little."

He gave her a shrewd look. "Did you know her son, Neil Hurly?"

Alison fought to keep her composure. She was an actress, after all—it should have been easy. But just the sound of Neil's name spoken by someone connected to the police made her face fall and her voice sound unsteady.

"A little," she said.

The guy noted her reaction. He had really turned the tables on her. "Did you go to school with him?"

"Why are you asking me all these questions?"

"I've only asked you a couple of questions. What's your name?"

"Alison."

"Alison what?"

"Alison. Who are you?"

"I've already told you who I am. My name's Eric Valence."

"I want to see some identification."

"I can show you my driver's license."

"No. How do I know you're with the police?"

"You could call them and check me out." He continued to study her. He knew she was worried. He had her over a barrel. "If you'd like to call the police, that is."

"I don't feel like doing anything right now except going home." She turned aside and stepped past him toward her car. He stopped her dead in her tracks with one little sentence.

"I know it wasn't Neil who burned to death in this house," he said.

"I don't know what you're talking about," she told the grass in front of her. He moved up and stood beside her.

"Yes, you do, Alison."

She looked at him out of the corner of her eye. "What do you want?"

"The truth. Who died here? Where's Neil?"

"Neil's dead."

"Where's his body?"

"I don't know."

"What did he die of?"

"Cancer."

Eric was surprised. "He had cancer?"

"Yeah. And if you don't believe me, ask his mother."

"That's just the point. I can't find his mother. Can you help me find her?"

"No. You don't want to do that. It would be a waste of time. She doesn't know anything. She thinks her son died in the fire that took place here."

Eric moved in front of her. "But you know differently. Tell me the story."

"No. Why should I? I don't even know you."

"But I know something about you. I know, for instance, that you were involved in a criminal deception."

Alison was indignant. "Are you threatening me?

'Cause if you are, you can go back to the police station and get your uncle and have him come arrest me." She pushed by him. "I don't need to listen to this anymore."

She had reached her car when he caught up with her again. "Look, Alison, I'm sorry. I shouldn't have said what I did. I do want to know what happened here, but I don't want to get you in trouble." He paused and awkwardly reached out toward her. "You look pretty upset. I want to help you. That's all. Please let me help?"

She was going to yell at him again when the words of the stranger at the lake came back to her.

*"You have asked for help, and someone will come. Trust this person."*

"How can you help me?" she asked quietly.

"I can tell you what I know. You can tell me what you know. We can join forces." He fidgeted awkwardly. "I'm smarter than I look. I'm good at figuring things out."

He sounded so pitifully sincere, she had to smile. "You look plenty smart to me, Eric." She opened the door of her car for him. "Let's go get some coffee. We can talk. But I don't know if you'll believe half of what I have to tell you."

They went to a Denny's Coffee Shop not far from Neil's old house. They got a booth in the corner. Both ordered coffee and pie. Eric confessed what his real relationship was to the police department, which seemed to her to be only that of a hopeful reject. But she was fascinated by how he had used their computers and his ingenuity in piercing through Neil's deception. He told her about the difference in the X-rays and promised to show them to her when she took him back to his car. Even without the stranger's advice, she felt she had to trust Eric. He was within a hairbreadth of exposing everything that had gone on before.

So she told him her tale, starting with the night of the concert and the dead man in the desert. She took Eric all the way through Neil's chain letters, up to the new letters and the death of Fran Darey. Occasionally Eric would interrupt to ask a specific question. Was there another car on the road when they hit the man? Was there a history of mental illness in Neil's family? Did anyone besides Tony see Neil die? How long after Fran's accident was it before the police arrived on the scene? Eric did indeed have a sharp mind. Many of the things he asked, Kipp hadn't even thought of. She answered each of his questions as carefully as she could. She was relieved that he believed her every word. She asked him about his faith in her when she was done.

"I know it must all sound pretty farfetched," she said. "I won't blame you if you think I'm crazy."

He sipped his coffee. He had hardly touched it while she spoke. "I believe you. You couldn't have made up a story like that. It's the most extraordinary thing I've ever heard."

"You asked a lot of questions. Tell me what you think."

He didn't hesitate. "I think you're in serious danger."

In a way it was good to have her beliefs confirmed. Yet his conviction brought her no relief. "You don't think Fran's death was an accident?" she asked.

"Unlikely. She died right on schedule."

Alison nodded weakly. "Fran was always worried about not being on schedule." She sniffed. "So what should we do? Should we go to the police?"

"I wouldn't, but then, I think I know more than most cops. *You* probably should. You need protection."

"Will we get in trouble if we go?"

"Will you go to jail? Probably not. This Tony guy will, though."

"Why him? We were all responsible."

"He was driving when the man was hit. He didn't report it. That's manslaughter." Eric paused. "What exactly is your relationship to Tony?"

"He's my boyfriend."

Eric blinked. "I see."

"I don't want him to go to jail. It's unacceptable." She reached out and touched Eric's hand. "You told me you'd keep everything I said confidential."

The news that she had a boyfriend seemed to have taken him back a step. "Yes, and I will keep my word. But you asked my advice, and I gave it to you. I think you should go to the police."

*"You know what I love? I love it that out of everyone in this group, you're the one who's making this suggestion. I just love it, Ali."*

"We can't do that. Not yet." She took a breath. "If you know more than most police, what would you do next if you were in my predicament?"

"If you're convinced that the new Caretaker is not someone in your group, then you should concentrate all your efforts on finding out who the man in the desert was. His identity is the missing link. There's a good chance you didn't even kill him. The fact that there was no other car in the area indicates that he might have been dumped there, already dead."

"But then why can't we tell the police that? Tony wouldn't have to go to jail."

Eric shook his head. "I know there was no other car in the area because I believe you. The police won't. You buried a dead man in an unmarked grave and didn't tell anybody about it for over a year. You'll have no credibility with the authorities."

"I see your point."

"Who the man was and how he died is crucial," Eric went on. "If he was murdered, the people who killed him might have had contact with Neil."

"I don't see the logic in that."

"It's obvious. Neil is dead. We must assume he's dead because your boyfriend says he is. But you're getting new chain letters, and they're similar to the ones Neil sent. Therefore, somebody outside the group must have seen Neil's chain letters. This is assuming no one else in your group has turned psychotic, which seems unlikely. It's possible the person who is sending them now is the same one who composed the first ones. Tell me, in the short time you spoke with Neil after you knew he was the Caretaker, did he at any time indicate he had help?"

*"I kept wondering and worrying and I tried, but this thing got in my head, and I couldn't get rid of it. I don't know where it came from. It was like a voice, saying this is true and this is a lie. It wouldn't shut up! I had to listen, and I did listen, and then . . . I did all this."*

"I don't think so," she whispered.

"You sound doubtful?"

"He did say something that indicated he was being influenced."

"How so?"

Alison repeated the remark Neil had made just before he collapsed into Tony's arms and was carried away. She added, "But it was just something that was in his head. It wasn't like he had a real physical accomplice."

"I'm not so sure about that," Eric disagreed. "If he was mentally ill from a tumor in his brain, then his accomplice could have dominated him in such a fashion that he would be unable, even at the end, to admit that he was working with someone. It's a theory is all. We'll have a better idea which direction to take if we find out who the man was."

"How do we do that?"

"We'll use the computer at the police station. We'll go through all the missing-person files for July of last year. But first tell me everything you remember about the man."

Alison gave him what details she could remember. He had been about thirty years old, Caucasian, handsome, and well dressed in a tan sport coat and light brown slacks. His eyes had been green. She remembered that fact because Neil's had also been green, and Tony had said later that he believed that was one of the reasons for Neil's intense identification with the man. Eric didn't take notes as he spoke. He seemed confident in the power of his memory.

As they were leaving the coffee shop to pick up Eric's car and drive to the police station, Eric asked a single question. "Do you know if Kipp definitely left town?" he asked.

"He promised he would," Alison said.

"Did he give anybody any idea where he was going?"

"Not that I know of. He might have told Tony. They're good friends."

"I hope he didn't," Eric muttered.

"Why not? Tony wouldn't tell anybody."

Eric opened the door to the coffee shop for her. "I hope you're right."

Alison found the ease with which Eric entered the police station and computer room unnerving. Apparently the uncle they had said hello to at the front desk made everything all right. Alison glanced around anxiously as Eric called up the appropriate files. The computer room was at the back of the station and deserted. Eric commented that until he came along, none of the people in the station knew how to use the computer.

"It's a pity," he said. "Computers are the detectives

of the future. With the right program and the right data they can uncover almost anything. Did I tell you I wrote several of the programs for this machine? We're going to use one of them now. Basically it's a filter. It'll eliminate all the people who can't be the man. That's important. You wouldn't believe how many people disappear in L.A. every month."

"Where do they all go?" Alison asked.

"Usually they're wives or husbands trying to get out of unhappy marriages."

"That's sad."

Eric glanced at her and pointed to the computer. "You read as many unsolved murder cases as I have, and you'll see how sad the world can be."

"Why do you do it?"

"What do you mean?" he asked.

"Why do you spend so much time focusing on the worst of humanity?"

The question caught him by surprise. It was as if he had never thought about it before. "I like the challenge of solving a difficult puzzle," he said finally.

"Then you don't do it to help people?"

"Of course I do," he said quickly. "I like people." He added shyly, "I like you, Alison."

She smiled and patted him on the back. "I like you, too, Eric. Now, get to work. The hourglass is running low."

*The time has come for your punishment. Listen closely, the hourglass runs low.*

A line from Neil's original chain letter. There was something about the cabin where she had met the strange guy that reminded her of Neil. But for the life of her she couldn't remember what it was.

Eric asked the computer to sort through the missing-persons files. It took longer than Alison expected. Eric explained that the files were not all in one place; he had to call up each batch individually. She brought him fresh coffee, which he said he appreciated greatly. He was an interesting guy. As he worked he told her the plot line of every Agatha Christie novel. There were a lot of them.

At close to eleven o'clock Eric finally had a list of six people who met the man's description. They were both relieved the list was short. The previous July must have been a slow month for runaways.

"Now what do we do with this list?" Alison asked.

"We can do a couple of things," Eric said. "We can look up the guys in the phone book and try to contact their families. We may even connect with some of the guys. The ones who went home. It would be helpful to eliminate a few of them. There's another program we can use. It takes a name and searches through all the specified editions of the *L.A. Times* for a mention of the name. The papers are all on microfilm and the computer scans them one page at a time. But it's a slow program. It would take all night to do all six of these people for the whole month of July."

"It's almost eleven," she said. "Do you want to call people now? You might wake them up."

"You're the one who's talking about hourglasses." Eric reached for the phone. "If I can get a nice person at Information it will speed the process up."

Eric got someone who was happy to help him. In fifteen minutes he had a list of numbers for four out of the six people. He called them. The first person hung up on him before he could get out two words. The second one—a woman—began to cry at the mention of the man on the list. Apparently he had been her husband and had vanished on a hunting trip, only to be found dead a month later outside the cave of a bear. The third one—another woman—laughed when she heard her guy's name. He had left her for another woman, she said, and she was happy to be rid of him. The fourth number rang and rang without a response.

"We still have the two people we couldn't get numbers for," Eric said. He read them out loud off their list—"James Whiting and Frank Smith. Christ, we would get a Smith. The program will be stopping constantly."

"Let's put James Whiting's name in first," Alison suggested.

"Good idea. I hope somebody wrote an article on him when he disappeared."

The program had not been running long—less than an hour—when it flagged that it had found James Whiting in the July 16 edition of the *Times*. The paper was not on the screen. The checking process was done internally. Eric had to call up the appropriate page. Alison was practically on top of him, she was so anxious.

Then she almost fainted to the floor.

There was a small article on James Whiting with a

picture of him. Alison remembered his handsome profile from when he lay flat on his back in the desert. It was ironic—in the photograph he had on his tan sport coat, the jacket they had buried him in. All that the picture was missing was the trail of blood at the corner of his mouth. She pointed at the screen with a shaking finger.

"That's him," she gasped. "That's the man."

"Are you sure?"

Alison swallowed. "I'm sure."

They read the article together.

### LOCAL BUSINESSMAN MISSING

*Thirty-three-year-old James Whiting, a local record store owner and resident of Santa Monica for the last fifteen years, has been missing from his home for over a week. His wife, Carol Whiting, has no explanation for his disappearance. The Whitings have two children, ages six and three. James Whiting's store, the Sound of Soul, is located on Westwood Boulevard and has been a local favorite for ten years. So far the police have no clues to his whereabouts. If anyone has any information regarding his disappearance, please contact the LAPD.*

Alison had to sit down. "He was married," she whispered. "He had two children. And we killed him and never told anybody."

"You don't know that you killed him," Eric said

quickly. "I told you there's an excellent chance he was murdered and then dumped in the desert."

Alison shook her head. Her eyes burned. "But we buried him and never told anybody. We could have told the police. Then his wife would have known what happened to him." She began to weep. "She probably sat home night after night wondering where her husband was. We could have at least let her know he wasn't coming home."

"You made a mistake," Eric said. "You were scared. It's done. The best thing you can do for his family right now is try to find out why he was in the middle of the desert in the middle of the night. And whether he was dead or alive when he got there." He handed her a tissue. "We have a lot of work ahead of us."

Alison wiped at her face. "What are we going to do now?"

"Go home and go to bed. James and Carol Whiting are not listed. We'll go to his record store in the morning. I know the place—it's still in business. We'll find his wife and talk to her. Don't worry—you won't have to say what happened in the desert. You can make up another story."

"But the article said she had no idea why her husband had disappeared," Alison said.

"These articles never say anything. She'll have things to tell us, you can be sure of that. If we can get them out of her." Eric turned back to the computer screen. He called up the missing-person file on James Whiting again. He put a hand to his chin and frowned.

"What is it?" she asked.

"What was the date of that concert?" he asked.

"It was the end of July," Alison said. "I could check if you need the exact date."

"I might need it. But note the date of this article? It's the middle of July. James was gone from home about two weeks before you supposedly hit him. Yet you said the blood coming out of his mouth was wet. Therefore he just died then, the night of the concert."

"That's interesting."

"Very. I wonder what James was doing during that missing two weeks—who he was with." Eric pointed at the screen. "This is the most hopeless-looking missing-person file I've ever seen. It has the barest of facts on James. It almost looks as if parts of it have been erased."

"Who would do that?"

Eric turned off the screen. "Maybe the person who killed him."

"But he wouldn't have had access to these records. Right?"

Eric appeared uneasy. "He shouldn't have. But whoever's behind these letters seems to be able to get ahold of whatever he wants. *Whoever* he wants."

Earlier Alison had driven Eric to his car, so they both had their cars with them. But Eric followed Alison back to her house. She protested that it was way out in the valley, but he insisted. When she parked in her driveway, he got out of his car to walk her to the front door. She had called her parents from the police station and told them she was at Brenda's house. They were worried about her, how she was handling the death of Fran. But they still wanted her to go to NYU. They thought the change of scenery would be good for her. She hadn't thought about school for a second since Fran had died.

Eric eyed the dark house. "Are you sure your parents are home?"

"I'd know if they went out of town." She touched his arm. "Really, Eric, I'll be all right. Nothing happens to you until your name comes up on the list. Oh, that's something I forgot to tell you. My name is the only one that isn't on the Caretaker's list."

Eric was startled. "Why didn't you tell me that?"

"I just forgot. Why? I'm sure the new Caretaker knows who I am."

"I'm sure he does. He knows everything else." Eric considered. "This worries me."

She laughed. "I would think it would reassure you. It's no fun being on one of these lists, I can tell you."

He forced a smile. "I understand. I have your number. I'll call you in the morning."

"All right." She started for her front door, then paused. Eric continued to stand in her driveway, thinking. She was happy to have his mind on this problem. He was more resourceful than anybody she knew. A wave of tenderness for him flowed through her. She turned and reached out to give him a quick hug and a kiss on the cheek. "You have sweet dreams," she said.

Her gesture surprised him. He smiled again, but

this time with pleasure. "How come it's always the prettiest girls who get in the worst trouble?" he asked.

"I think it's because of the guys they hang out with." She messed up his hair and walked away. "Good night, Eric. Call me early."

"Good night, Ali."

# CHAPTER TEN

Sitting in his car down the street from Alison's house, Tony and Sasha watched Alison hug and kiss the handsome young stranger. And Tony felt a part of him die inside. But this part, as it died, didn't cease to hurt. It just rotted, and in the few seconds that Alison hugged the other guy the filth of it spread through his whole body until he could hardly breathe. Sasha sat silently beside him in the dark. If she knew he was in agony, she gave no sign of it. Tony had to close his eyes. His grief lay on top of him like a boulder, and his anger rocked his soul to its very foundation. That cheating bitch! How long had this been going on? Probably from the time he had first said hello to her. He opened his eyes and watched as the guy walked back to his car. He wondered if the guy had given his girl a feel while his eyes had been shut.

*My girl. She's everybody's girl. Whoever wants her can have her.*

The guy drove away without noticing them. Tony made a mental note of the guy's car—a red Honda

Civic. He had a sinking feeling he'd see that car again. He reached for the key in his ignition.

"I should take you home," he muttered.

Sasha stopped him. "I didn't know we'd see this."

"But you wanted to come here." The streetlight beside them was burned out. He stared at her in the dark. They hadn't sat there long before Alison returned with her date. "Why?"

Her green eyes were on him. "Sometimes a girl gets a feeling about someone just by hearing about her. I had a feeling about Alison."

"What do you feel about her now?"

"That she's a whore."

Tony nodded and started the car. "My sentiment exactly."

The drive back to Sasha's apartment seemed to take an eternity. Had Tony been alone, he might have driven off the road, or into the oncoming traffic. Yeah, better to go out in a ball of fire and take a few others with him. Then, at least, he'd get himself on the front page of the paper. His devastation felt complete. He didn't want to live. He didn't want to breathe.

But he did want to get back at Alison.

Sasha invited him up to her apartment. He begged off, pleading exhaustion, but she insisted. Soon he was sitting on her couch, drinking coffee beside her. He took it scalding black, like her, and felt it burn as it went down. He sat staring at the carpet on her floor. It was gray—the color of his universe. He could think of absolutely nothing to say. Sasha reached over and rubbed his shoulder.

"I think it's time for that massage I promised you," she said.

"It's too late. Another time."

Her fingers worked into his muscles for a moment, then she stood. "You need it now. I'll get my table. I'll set it up out here."

He let her do what she wanted. She had a mind of her own, that was for sure. That goddamn Alison—all this time she'd been pretending to love him, when really he was just another body to jump on. She had made him feel like a piece of meat. She had probably screwed a dozen different guys since they'd started going out. It made him want to vomit to think about it.

Sasha came back with her massage table and began to unfold the legs. "I bought this table especially to work on people," she said. "It cost me four hundred dollars. But it was worth it. You can fall asleep on it if you want, it's so comfortable. Why don't you take off your clothes?"

He looked up. "What?"

"Take off your clothes. I can't give you a massage with them on. I use oil."

He glanced at his watch. It was two-thirty in the morning. "Do I have to take them all off?"

She was enjoying herself. "If you want me to do all of you. Don't be shy. I'll get you a towel to cover yourself."

She left the room and returned with a towel, and then went into the bathroom. He decided if he was going to undress, now was the time. He took off

111

everything except his underwear. Then he lay facedown on the table and covered his lower body with the towel, his bare feet sticking out the bottom. The apartment was warm, and he was as comfortable as a man with a broken heart and a slut for a girlfriend could be. He glanced up as Sasha returned to the living room wearing a white nightgown and no shoes or socks. She carried an unlabeled bottle of lavender-colored oil in her right hand.

"Are you all right?" she asked.

"I'm fine." He lay down again. He heard her pour out a little oil and rub it briskly between her palms. She laid her hands gently on his back, and her touch was soft and greasy. He sighed involuntarily with pleasure. She began to rub the oil into his skin.

"Does that feel good?" she asked.

"Yes."

"Are you still thinking about Alison?"

"No," he lied.

"You're lying. That's OK. You won't be thinking about her soon." Her hands shifted under the towel, and before he could stop her, she had pulled off his underwear and then re-covered him.

"Hey," he protested.

"You're too uptight," she said, returning to her exquisite massaging of the muscles along his spine. As her fingers probed deeper, he realized just how tight he was. His back was one huge spastic muscle. It was funny how Alison had never offered to rub his back before. There were a lot of things she had never done for him that Sasha was already doing. Like being a friend when times were tough, rather than a cheating bitch. He just couldn't get that phrase out of his head.

*Cheating bitch. Cheating bitch. Goddamn bitch.*

Swear words had been invented for times like this.

"I appreciate this," he mumbled.

"You just relax and go on appreciating it. Go to sleep if you want. Alison's nothing. Forget her. She's already forgotten you."

"I want to forget her," Tony whispered. He let her touch travel all over his skin, the scented oil sinking deeper into his pores. Every now and then she'd lightly scratch him, making the nerves at the base of his spine moan with pleasure. But he didn't get sexually aroused. He was too exhausted. It occurred to him, just before he passed out, that the oil smelled like the rest of the apartment. It wasn't a particularly pleasant odor. He figured she must have got it at the hospital. He'd have to tell her to use something else—next time.

Tony went to sleep.

The nightmare started where it had left off.

He was back in the vast abyss of despair. The place of red and purple lights, foul smells, and far-off cries. The pit of loud thunder and watchful eyes. He was approaching the huge dark wall, and this time he could see it clearly. It seemed to divide the very universe in two. But what a universe it was. On one side was pain. On the other was only more pain. What choice could he make? All he knew was he didn't want to join the tortured people. He knew they were trapped for eternity.

As he closed in on the wall, he saw that it was riddled with black portals or holes. There was no wind, yet he felt himself being sucked toward one of them, and he was unable to stop himself. His panic grew as the narrow opening swelled into a maw capable of swallowing a battleship. He drifted inside, and the lights and thunder were lost behind him. He was in a vacuum of blackness. Yet the sulfuric fumes had thickened. He felt himself smothering and prayed for it to end, but even as he did so he knew he was in a place where prayers were no longer heard.

But was that true? Or was it just another of *their* lies?

Them. The Caretakers.

Suddenly, in the black void, he could see into a bedroom lit by moonlight flooding into rectangular windows. He saw the place as a slice of reality cut out of his space of nonexistence. But the slice grew as he moved toward it, and soon he was inside the bedroom, although he could still sense the void behind him, waiting for him to return. On the bed lay his friend Kipp, snoring peacefully.

"Kipp," Tony said softly. "Can you hear me? Wake up. Where am I?"

His friend stirred and sat up. "Hello? Who's there?"

"It's me, Kipp. Tony. I'm right here."

Kipp didn't hear him. But he heard something. "Hello? Mary Lou?" Kipp climbed out of the bed in his underwear and walked to the bedroom door, passing right by Tony. Kipp peeked out into the hallway. It was then Tony noticed the noise that had awakened Kipp. He had to assume Kipp hadn't heard him since he didn't seem able to see him.

*Am I a ghost? Am I dead?*

The noise was coming from downstairs. Kipp started to call out to his aunt again—Tony remembered that Kipp's aunt's name was Mary Lou—when he decided to go investigate the noise himself. Tony didn't like that idea. He ran after Kipp as he made his way down the stairs.

"Don't go outside," Tony said. "One of the Caretakers might be out there. Kipp! Listen to me!"

But Kipp wasn't listening. Still in his underwear, he walked to the front door and opened it and peeked outside. The noise appeared to be coming from the garage. It sounded like someone scratching a rake across the hood of a car.

"Who's there?" Kipp called.

"It's one of them!" Tony pleaded, standing at his friend's side. "Don't go out there."

"Hello?" Kipp called again. He went outside. Tony tried to grab hold of his arms, but he could have been trying to grab his own reflection in a mirror. Kipp strode across the overgrown lawn and entered the garage through a side door.

"Oh, God, stop!" Tony cried.

The raking noise inside the garage had stopped. Kipp fumbled for a light, but when he threw the switch, the garage remained dark. Kipp frowned. His eyes grew wide when he noticed that the paint on one side of his aunt's car had been largely scratched away.

"It doesn't matter," Tony hissed. "Get out of here."

Kipp heard a sound coming from the bowels of the garage. Brave fool that he was, he walked toward it. "Hello?" Kipp said.

A wave of liquid came flying out of the dark directly at Kipp. In a moment he was drenched, and a metal bucket clamored to the concrete floor in front of him. Kipp hardly had a second to register what was happening before a wooden match flared to life, scraped along the side of the ruined car by a figure wrapped in black shadow. Tony's nose was working fine, and the air stunk of gasoline.

"Kipp!" Tony screamed even though Kipp couldn't hear his words.

The shadowy figure tossed the burning match toward Kipp. It bounced harmlessly off his chest without igniting the gasoline, but it landed in the puddle at his feet. Kipp stared down at the tiny orange flame, amazed, but only for a second before he was transformed into a human torch. The flames whipped up his legs all the way to his hair, and the scream that poured out of Kipp's throat rent Tony's heart. Kipp thrashed up and down like a demented scarecrow for several seconds in the worst imaginable pain a human being could experience.

Tony tried to grab him, to hold him, to do something for him. But he couldn't, and it didn't matter anyway. It was too late. Kipp fell to his blackened knees, and his screams began to die as the flesh surrounding his mouth was peeled away in crisp layers. Yet the screams didn't stop for Tony. After he watched his friend slowly die, he was suddenly back in the black portal that ran between the two hells. And the screams of those on the far side of the wall were no longer so distant, no longer so different from human wails. In fact, they sounded very much the same as Kipp did as he passed out of the world of the living. Filled with anguish, devoid of hope, forever forsaken. . . .

Tony opened his eyes and found himself staring up at a strange ceiling. At first he hadn't the slightest idea where he was. Nor did he care. He was just happy the nightmare was over. Never in his worst dreams had he experienced anything so terrible.

Tony moved his head to the side and saw Sasha curled up in a sleeping ball on the couch. The entire evening came back to him in a flash. The relief of waking from the nightmare faded as he remembered Alison's betrayal. How could she have been kissing another man when she said she still loved him? She was worse than the Harlot of Bablyon. She was a whore. Sasha had said it right.

Tony sat up and shivered. Except for the towel around his waist, he was naked. He couldn't imagine how Sasha had managed to turn him over without waking him. But he'd been under a lot of stress lately. He was exhausted. He had to get home and into bed.

The images from his nightmare wouldn't leave him, though. Watching Kipp burn had seemed so real. Tony wondered why he had dreamed Kipp was at his aunt's house, although it would be a logical place for Kipp to run. Kipp had not told anyone where he was going. Tony tried to remember the aunt's last name. It was Felix, yeah, and she lived in Santa Barbara. Hugging the towel around his waist, Tony slipped off the massage table and tiptoed to the phone in the kitchen. He was being silly, he knew, but it couldn't hurt to give Kipp a call and see how he was doing, assuming he was at his aunt's. Tony picked up the receiver and dialed Information. The aunt was listed, and a moment later he had Kipp on the phone. It sounded as if he had woken his friend up. Made sense—it was the middle of the night. Tony didn't mind. It was such a relief to hear Kipp's voice.

"Yeah, what is it, Tony?" Kipp mumbled.

"I wanted to see if you were all right."

Kipp yawned. "I'm fine. How did you know I was here?"

"Just a guess. I'm sorry to wake you. Go back to sleep. I'll call you in a couple of days."

"Everything cool there?"

"Everything's cool," Tony told him. "Good night. You got your night-light on?" It was a reference to a remark Kipp had made just before Neil had kidnapped him. Kipp laughed quietly.

"Sure do," Kipp said. "Happy dreams, buddy."

Tony set the phone down. He walked back into the living room, still clutching his towel, and found Sasha sitting on the couch. A tunnel of moonlight cut through a nearby window and landed on her legs. But her face remained dark. Her green eyes—he could hardly see them.

"What's the matter?" she asked.

"Nothing."

"Where are you going?"

"Nowhere." He reached for his pants.

"You must be going somewhere." She stood and smoothed her nightgown over her sleek hips. "You're getting dressed."

"I have to go home." He couldn't find his underwear. What had she done with it? She strode across the room and put her hands on his shoulders, interrupting his search.

"Why?" she asked.

"You don't want me staying the night."

In response she reached up and kissed him on the lips. A hard wet kiss. And he kissed her back, and her hand went around the back of his neck, into his hair, and began to pull at his blond strands until they hurt. He yanked away from her and took a breath. She mocked him with a naughty smile.

"Why can't you stay?" she asked again.

Her lips had tasted like pure pleasure. Suddenly he couldn't think of a single reason. "All right," he said. "But I've been told I snore."

She took his hand and led him toward her bedroom. "Who told you that? Alison?"

He hesitated. "Yeah."

"Is that who you were calling?"

"No. I was calling a friend of mine—Kipp Coughlan. He's staying with his aunt in Santa Barbara for a few days."

"Why?"

"There's some trouble that he's trying to stay out of. It's a long story."

They entered her bedroom, and she let go of his hand and pulled back the covers. He couldn't believe what he was doing. He was about to make love to a girl other than Alison. He should have felt no guilt, after what he had seen that night. But he did—plenty of guilt. He felt scared, too, and he didn't know why. Sasha took his hand again and pulled him onto the bed and kissed him some more. These kisses were softer, slower, like the strokes of her massaging fingers when they were not probing deep into his sore body. She scratched her fingernails across his hard belly.

"Tell me your long story," she whispered.

"You don't want to hear it."

"But I do. It's on your mind. I want to put your mind at ease." She nibbled on his ear with her wet teeth. "I want to make you happy."

Tony began to talk. He didn't know why. Maybe because he was exhausted. Maybe because he was in the arms of a beautiful girl. He talked a lot. He told her about Neil and the original chain letters. He even told her about the new Caretaker, and the horrible nightmares he'd been having. Sasha listened silently between caresses and kisses. When he was done, she just nodded and touched him all over, and kissed him so deep he felt as if he were being swallowed whole. But she didn't let him make love to her. She kept her nightgown on the entire night, and eventually he fell asleep and dreamed no more.

# CHAPTER ELEVEN

*E*ric called Alison early Sunday morning. He had good news and bad news. The new owner of James Whiting's record store was not going to be in till Tuesday, and the help refused to give out his home number. That was the bad news. The good news was that James Whiting's brother was the guy who had bought the store. If anyone knew where James had been during those missing two weeks, it should be he, Eric thought. Eric told Alison to keep her head low and call him if anything happened between then and Tuesday. All day Sunday Alison tried to reach Tony, with no luck. His parents didn't know where he was. That made her worry all the more.

Come Monday there was still no sign of Tony.

He didn't even show up for Fran's funeral.

They buried Fran in the same cemetery where Neil had been laid to rest. Of course, Neil had been alive at the time of his funeral, and they had unknowingly spent the afternoon mourning the remains of James Whiting. Such could not be said for Fran. As the doctor at the hospital had said, she was as dead as they came. Alison stood dressed in black beside Brenda and couldn't be free of the idea that Fran lay only a couple feet away without her head properly attached. The attending minister spoke about the valley of the shadow of death and lying down in green pastures to rest beside clear waters. It all sounded like a badly written fairy tale to Alison. If there was a God, he was keeping his address secret. Maybe he didn't want to get a chain letter. Alison was beginning to believe the Caretaker was working for the devil. She had had a hellish dream the night before, filled with weird colored lights, sick smells, and tortured souls.

The funeral finally came to an end, and Alison hugged and kissed Fran's parents and told them if there was anything she could do . . . What a futile offer. What could she do for them? Be their daughter? Fran had been their only child. It was all so sad.

Alison said goodbye to Brenda and her own parents and drove home by herself. But as she had on Saturday, she passed by her usual off-ramp and headed for the mountains. An hour and a half later she found herself walking beside the lake where she had met the intriguing stranger. She went to the door of his cabin and knocked repeatedly. There was no answer. She tried the knob, and the door swung in easily. But the inside was not as she had remembered it, not exactly. There was the same wood stove, the same black kettle sitting on top of it. But the place was filled with dust and cobwebs, as if it had been months since anyone had lived there. It made her wonder whether her encounter with the stranger had been a dream—or worse, a hallucination. Yet she knew in her heart that it had been neither. She wondered if she should discuss the matter with Eric. She'd have liked to tell Tony about the mystical encounter. Where could he be? That morning his parents had said he was out doing errands.

Night was falling when Alison finally returned home. She sat in her room and read a book before going to bed. She had trouble concentrating on the story, and when the heroine died unexpectedly at the end, she felt nothing. She was too worried about which of her friends was going to die next. Thank God Kipp had done what he promised and gone away without telling anyone where he was. She had cursed God that morning, and now she was thanking him. She hoped he gave her no more reasons to destroy her faith.

But God did. Or rather, the Caretaker did.

Another call shook her awake in the middle of the night. She turned on the light before picking it up. She knew the news couldn't be good.

"Hello?" she said.

"Ali." It was Brenda, broken and tearful.

"What's happened? Is he dead? He can't be dead, dammit!"

Brenda moaned. "He was at his aunt's. Tony just called me. The Caretaker got him there. Soaked him with gasoline and set him on fire. Oh, Ali, Kipp's gone."

"Do you want me to come over?" Alison asked.

"No." Brenda's voice suddenly sounded distant. "I'm next on the list. There'll be a letter for me in the morning. Stay away from me."

"But we have to have another meeting of the group. We have to go to the police. Brenda?"

Her girlfriend had hung up. Alison quickly dialed Eric. She woke him up, but he didn't sound mad. She told him what had happened. He cursed softly.

"Tell me the order of the people on the list again?" he asked.

"It's Brenda, Joan, and Tony. Brenda will probably get a letter in the mail tomorrow, the way this Caretaker works."

"You say you guys are going to have a meeting tomorrow?"

"I'm going to try to organize one," she said.

"Make it for the afternoon. I want to come, but I have to do some things in the morning first."

"I don't know if the gang will let you come."

"It doesn't matter. You tell me when and where it is, and I'll show up. They'll have to listen to what I have to say."

"You're going to tell them we have to go to the police, aren't you? We have to put a stop to this."

Eric was evasive. "I hope I'll have a better idea tomorrow about what to recommend."

"Where are you going in the morning?"

"The record store. It's more on my side of town, so you don't need to go. Just stay home and rest. The newspaper office, too. I want to see if I can trace who's been placing these ads."

They had tried a similar tactic with Neil's chain letters. They had been unsuccessful. "Good luck," she said.

124

"Once you have the meeting set, call and leave the information on my answering machine. And, Ali?"

"Yes."

"We're going to stop this bastard."

"How can you be so sure?" she asked.

"He'll make a mistake. They always do. He may have made one already."

"What?"

He hesitated. "Let me talk to you about it tomorrow."

They said their goodbyes and Alison set down the phone. Tony had called Brenda but hadn't called her. That said a lot about the condition of their relationship. Reluctantly she picked up the phone again and dialed his number. Someone answered quickly on his end, but didn't speak.

"Hello?" she said. "Tony? Are you there, Tony?"

She could hear breathing. It could be his. Then behind him she could make out faint whispering. This did not belong to Tony.

It was a girl.

"Tony?" she cried.

The phone clicked in her ear, and she heard nothing but a dial tone.

# CHAPTER TWELVE

*T*he gang met at twelve sharp in the park beside the rocket ship. Once there had been seven. Now there were only four: Brenda, Joan, Alison, and Tony. Alison had had to get Joan to call Tony about the meeting. Tony wasn't returning her calls. Tony sat on the slide across from her and stared at her as if he had never seen her before. But he knew who she was. She had tried to give him a comforting hug and tell him how sorry she was about what had happened to Kipp, but he had brushed her away with a sharp move of his arm. Life was wonderful.

Brenda had received a letter in the morning mail. Kipp's name had gone the way of Fran's—into nothingness. There was an ad in the Personals section of the *Times* for Brenda. Decoded it read:

> Cut off your trigger finger and give it to Joan with her letter.

Trigger finger? Brenda didn't even own a gun. But Joan's dad did. He was a cop. The gang wanted to start the meeting, but Alison stalled them for a few minutes. She was waiting for Eric to arrive. She had called and left the information he requested on his machine. He didn't disappoint her. Out of nowhere he came walking over a grass hill and strode into the center of the group. Joan and Brenda stared at him, amazed. Strangely enough, Tony didn't seem surprised to see him. Tony shook his head and spit on the ground.

"Hi," Eric said. "I'm a friend of Alison's. I know about the chain letters, but please don't get mad at her. I made her tell me what she knew."

Joan turned to Alison. "Are you out of your mind to bring in a stranger? Don't we have enough problems as it is?"

Brenda had been a decent shade of white before Eric's arrival. Now she could have tried out for the lead role in a play about Casper the Ghost. "Ali," she begged. "What's got into you?"

"Eric discovered that it wasn't Neil who burned to death in the fire in June," Alison said quickly. "He came to me, I didn't go to him. But I'm glad he's here. He's an amateur sleuth, and he's better than most professionals. He's discovered who the man in the desert was."

"Who?" Tony asked tonelessly.

"James Whiting," Eric said. He looked at Tony. "May I sit down?"

Tony eyed him with barely concealed hatred. "Sure."

Eric sat down near Alison. "I'm here to help you guys," he said. "What Alison said is true. She didn't approach me, I approached her. My uncle works for the LAPD. I was going through the police files and stumbled on the fact that Neil had been identified by an emerald ring after burning to death in a raging fire. I knew an emerald would melt in such a fire and figured there had to be something wrong. That started me on my investigation. So far I have kept the confidence of your group. I've told no one about the chain letters."

Tony was amused. "You're connected to the police. Great."

"Only in an unofficial capacity," Eric said smoothly. "But let's not argue about whether I should be here or not. I'm here, and I want to help you out of this predicament."

"What can you do?" Joan asked sarcastically.

Eric turned the left side of his head toward her. "What?"

"Can't you hear?" Joan asked.

"I can hear," Eric said. "Please repeat your question?"

Joan was mean. "You can't help us. You can't even understand what we say."

"I can give you advice," Eric said. "I can point out certain facts that maybe you overlooked. I'll point out one right now. But first I have to ask a question. Who in this group knew where Kipp had gone?"

"None of us," Brenda said. "That was the point of his leaving."

"Then how did the Caretaker know where to find him?" Eric asked. No one answered. Eric scanned the group. "Someone must have known. How about you, Tony? You were closest to him."

Tony surprised them all. "I knew he was at his aunt's."

"How?" Alison exclaimed.

Tony ignored the question.

"How did you know?" Brenda had to ask.

"I called him on the phone there and he answered," Tony said simply.

"But how did you know to call him there?" Joan asked.

Tony shrugged. "I don't know."

"You're going to have to do better than that," Eric said.

Tony chuckled and spit again. "I don't have to do anything."

"All right," Eric said diplomatically. "Could you tell us if you told anybody else where Kipp went?"

Tony flashed a fake smile. "I don't remember."

"Tony!" Brenda protested. "For God's sake, tell him if you did."

Tony hardened. "Why? This guy's an asshole. He's here to help us? He's here to give us advice? What kind of advice do you have for us, Mr. Amateur Sleuth?"

"I suppose the simplest thing for you to do now would be to go to the police," Eric said philosophically.

"If we do, we'll go to jail," Joan said with no strength in her protest. Indeed, it seemed as if Joan was considering the possibility as they spoke.

"Better to be in jail for a little while than to die," Eric said.

Brenda spoke in a faltering voice. "But this Caretaker could get us even there. Tony wouldn't have told anyone where Kipp was, even if he did know. In jail we could be more helpless."

"That's not true," Alison said. "With the police we'll be safe."

"Safe?" Brenda asked, and her voice cracked altogether. Her opinion of the Caretaker had changed a hundred and eighty degrees since their last meeting, which didn't surprise Alison. "Who can protect us from this monster? I tell you no one can. He pulled Kipp's whereabouts out of thin air. He went there in the middle of the night, lured my boyfriend into the garage, soaked him with gasoline, and then lit him on fire. He did all this without leaving a trace. Tell me what kind of man could do that? Not one that's human, that's who!"

Her words sent a shock through the group, and they fell silent. They had thought such a thing—that their assailant might be of supernatural origin—when Neil's letters had been coming. Of course, they realized how silly they'd been—later. But not much later, because right now, to Alison, there was a ring of truth to what Brenda was suggesting. Eric did not agree.

"Kipp was killed by someone in a human body," Eric said. "There is a rational explanation for everything. It often takes time and hard work to find it, but the truth usually comes out in the end." Eric reached over and patted Alison on the leg. "Now, I went to the paper and the record store this morning. I found out that—"

"I'm getting out of here!" Tony exclaimed, jumping to his feet and hustling toward the parking lot. Alison got up and ran after him. She went alone. She didn't catch up to him until they were halfway to the cars, at the top of a grassy bluff. He threw off her arm with a cruel swing of his.

"Tony?" she cried. "You have to stop this. You have to talk to me!"

"I don't talk to whores," he muttered, plowing forward.

Alison's breath caught in her throat. "How can you call me that?"

He whirled on her, and his voice and face were savage. He was like a man possessed. "I was there Saturday night when you were kissing your new boyfriend. I saw it all. But that's OK because you see, I wasn't alone. I had a new girl with me." He stabbed a finger in the direction of his car at the bottom of the hill. "I have her with me today."

A young woman with long maroon hair sat in the passenger seat. She nodded and climbed slowly out of Tony's car. She did not approach them, but stood there leaning with one hand braced on the side of the car, dressed entirely in black. She was extraordinarily attractive, but a cruel light seemed to emanate from her straight into Alison's heart. It was almost as if the strange girl were challenging Alison to a duel with invisible steel knives. In fact, Alison felt as if one of the girl's knives had already struck home. The pain in her heart was overwhelming.

"I did not cheat on you," she whispered to Tony.

"Fine," Tony said coldly. "I didn't cheat on you, either, when I slept with Sasha. All's fair in love." This time he spat on her. "Bitch."

She watched him walk away. The girl—Sasha—didn't climb back into the car until Tony arrived. Then the girl gave Alison one last stab with her weird green eyes and got in beside Tony. Alison watched them kiss. Sasha squashed so hard against Tony's face it looked as if she were trying to eat him alive. Then Alison watched them both laugh and drive off.

Eric walked up to Alison. He offered her a handkerchief, which she took to wipe off Tony's spit from the side of her face. His saliva had a funny smell to it. It reminded her of biology class.

"I'm sorry," he said.

"So am I," she whispered.

"The girls are waiting back at the rocket ship to hear what I've discovered," Eric said. "But I don't know if I want to tell now. This group is extremely unstable. I don't know if we can trust any of them."

"That girl is bad."

"Pardon?"

Alison looked at him. "That girl is bad."

Eric blinked. "I can see why you don't like her."

Alison shook her head and sighed. She felt as if she were already trapped in the Caretaker's box. She couldn't help wondering if everything that had just happened hadn't been planned in advance.

"What did you find out?" she asked.

"Nothing from the paper. They protect the identity of anybody who places an ad, no matter how weird. But the police might be able to go back there later and learn something."

"What about at the record store?" she asked.

"I spoke to James's brother. He was elusive. He

knew stuff, but he wasn't talking. He did give me the home address of his sister-in-law."

"James Whiting's wife?"

"Yes. Want to go have a talk with her?"

Alison stared in the direction Tony had disappeared. He had slept with another girl. Her Tony. It was hard to imagine. It was horrible to think about. He must have been put under a spell.

"I want to talk to her right now," Alison replied.

# CHAPTER THIRTEEN

**M**rs. Carol Whiting was not at home when they tried the front door of the tiny redbrick house in Santa Monica. Or maybe she was and her brother-in-law had warned her that he had given out her address. Alison asked Eric what story he had fed the brother-in-law, but Eric was evasive. He just said he had his "ways."

There was nothing to do but hang out near there until the woman came home. Eric took her to a restaurant, but she couldn't even eat her salad. They tried the house again, found no one there, and then Eric took her to a sci-fi film about a future society of humans who wanted to be robots. Alison fell asleep in the movie. She hadn't slept the previous night after hearing about Kipp's death. She did sleep now through two showings of the movie. When Eric woke her it was ten o'clock at night. He asked if she'd been having nightmares. Apparently she had often kicked and clawed at the air while unconscious. But she'd had no dreams that she could recall. All she knew was that her long nap had done little to refresh her.

They went to the woman's house once more.

She was at home and opened the door for them.

"Yes?" she said. "Can I help you?"

She was a short, plump woman with smooth dark features and a nervous twitch in her right eye. She couldn't have been thirty, but she had a streak of gray that split her short hair in two. She looked tired.

"Hi," Eric began. "My name's Tom and this is Amy and we're here to—"

"Talk to you about your missing husband," Alison interrupted.

Eric stared at her in shock. He had told her ahead of time to leave everything to him. But she was tired of deception. The woman had backed up a step.

"I don't understand," she said.

"We know what happened to your husband," Alison said. "We'd like to tell you the whole story. May we come in?"

"You knew Jim?" the woman asked, uncertain.

"No," Alison said. "But I was one of the people who helped bury him."

The woman shuddered. "Who are you?" she asked.

Alison reached out and touched the woman's hand. At first the woman flinched, but as she looked into Alison's eyes, she seemed to relax. Maybe she could see that Alison, too, had been to hell and had yet to come back.

"Please," Alison said. "We mean you no harm."

She studied them for a moment longer before opening the door wider. "Come in," she said.

The woman insisted that they call her Carol. Her brother-in-law had not warned her that they were coming over. Just the same, her children were not at home. They were at a sister's house, which was probably a good thing. Alison figured they wouldn't have got inside with the kids around. Carol was making herself coffee and asked if they would like a cup. They said sure. Carol fussed over them. She was obviously dying to hear what they had to say, but at the same time she was doing everything to postpone it.

There was a picture of the man on the piano. Jim.

When the three of them were seated comfortably in the living room, with Eric positioned with his good ear toward Carol, Alison described what had happened the summer before in the desert after the concert. She kept her story focused on that night alone. She didn't go into the chain letters or Neil's madness. Sitting across from her, Eric began to relax. As she approached the part where they buried the man, she began to cry softly. It was no act. She couldn't get over the fact that she was talking to the man's wife. Carol cried with her as she tried to explain why they hadn't gone to the police.

"We thought of you," Alison said. "I mean, we didn't know if you even existed. But we knew the man must have family somewhere. We thought we could send an anonymous letter to the police explaining what had happened. But we were afraid it would be traced back to us." Alison wiped at her face. She had shed a lot of tears lately. One of these days they were going to dry up. But today was not that day. Another flood burst out as she thought of covering the man with dirt. "We didn't mean to kill him. It was an accident. We were driving with our lights out and then we hit him and that was that. I'm so sorry, Carol. I can't tell you how sorry I am. All this time you must have wondered what happened to him."

Carol surprised her by reaching out and hugging her, comforting her. This crazy teenager who had destroyed her husband's life. It made no sense to Alison until Carol spoke.

"I have always wondered what happened to Jim's body," Carol said gently. "I would lie awake at night wondering where he lay. But I knew he was dead. I have always known who killed him. Don't be so hard on yourself, Alison. Jim was dead when you and your friends ran over his body."

Alison stared at her in disbelief. "Are you sure?"

Carol sat back in her seat. "Maybe I should tell you my story. It'll put your mind at ease." She put her hand to her forehead. "But those are days I don't care to remember."

"Tell us what you feel comfortable with," Alison said.

Carol shrugged. "I guess I'll have to start at the beginning. Jim and I were married eight years before he met Charlene. We had a happy life. He had the record store and business was good. We both had the children to play with and love. I was finishing my master's in education at UCLA. I remember the first night Jim mentioned Charlene to me. We were sitting in bed at night reading. He just tossed out her name. He said she was a pretty girl who regularly came into the store and was always asking him to order CDs of bands he'd never heard of. Groups like Dried Blood and Black Sex—real sicko groups. I remember Jim saying that Charlene seemed like such a nice girl to be into crap like that. I just grunted. Jim had lots of odd customers. And that was the last I heard of Charlene for a long time.

"Several months went by and Jim began to change in small ways. He became more impatient with the children and snapped at me frequently. I'm not saying Jim was a saint before this change occurred, but he had always been a nice guy. He really was, and I'm not just saying that because I was his wife. He didn't wish anybody any harm. But his mood had turned sour, and I didn't know how to shake him out of it. He began to suffer from insomnia and took to spending longer hours at the store. It got so that he almost never came home, even when the store was closed. You must think I was pretty stupid, huh? I couldn't see that he was having an affair. But at the time I was worried that he was sick. He'd always been a bit chubby, but now he was definitely on the slim side. I'd put a home-cooked meal in front of him and he'd just pick.

"Then I caught him snorting cocaine in our bathroom one day. I had come home early from school. I was shocked. The music business is full of drugs, but Jim wasn't that kind of guy. He never put anything harmful in his body. Finally, I thought, I understood the changes that were happening in him. He told me that he was barely into the stuff, that it was just a weekend habit. But he was obviously an addict. I checked our bank account. I always let Jim handle the business side of our lives. I was sick when I learned that we were broke. Jim had blown all our savings on drugs. When I confronted him with what I'd found, he promised that he'd get help. I went with him to several clinics, and he seemed to be ready to enter one when I made another shocking discovery.

"I was digging in my garden when I smelled something peculiar. I dug a little deeper and found a green trash bag filled with the remains of desecrated animals. There were dogs and cats and even a skunk. And all of them had been beheaded and their fur shaved with strange symbols. Not for a second did I think they had anything to do with Jim, but when I told him about what I had found, it was all there on his face. He had done those things to those animals! I couldn't believe it. Was this the man I had married? He was behaving like a psycho. I took the children and left for my sister's.

"But Jim called me every night and begged me to come back. He told me he had gotten involved with bad people but that he was getting away from them. He mentioned Charlene's name as one of them. I didn't know who she was until he reminded me. But the way he said her name made me suspicious. I asked him if he was having an affair with her, and when he didn't answer right away, I knew where I stood. That was one thing I wouldn't put up with—unfaithfulness. I swore I'd never see him again and hung up on him. But two minutes later I was missing him worse than I ever had in my life. I drove over to our house and got there just as Charlene was arriving.

"She was pretty. I could see that from where I was sitting in my car up the block. They didn't see me. I watched as she dragged Jim out of the house and into her car. She was laughing all the time like a teenager. They drove away and I followed. They got off the freeway in a section of town where the gangs are very active. I knew I was risking my life just to go there. They parked outside a shabby warehouse, and the girl dragged Jim inside. I keep using the word *dragged*. It was obvious Jim didn't want to go. I'm not saying that to protect him, either. I assumed Charlene was into drugs and that she was taking my husband to meet her connection.

"I sat outside that old warehouse for hours, well into the night. But they never reappeared, and the characters walking by on the street really scared me. Finally I had to go back to my sister's. But I noted exactly where the warehouse was, and the next day I returned there with the police."

"The police let you go inside the warehouse with them?" Eric broke in, surprised.

"Not at first. Two of them checked out the warehouse while I waited in the patrol car. When they came back outside, their faces were white. One of them had to run into the alley and vomit against the wall. They told me there was nobody inside, and that I didn't want to see what was in there. But, of course, I did want to see. My husband was involved here. I jumped out of the car and ran inside before they could stop me."

"It was a meeting place for a satanic cult?" Eric said.

Carol raised an eyebrow. "How did you know?"

140

"It fits the pattern," Eric said. "Please go on."

Carol's face showed extreme revulsion. "It stank in there beyond belief. There was dried blood everywhere, and blood that was not so dry. Animal entrails and skins lay everywhere. The walls and floor were covered with bizarre symbols. Many had been painted in blood. There were half-burnt black candles on the floor, as if someone had been celebrating a black mass. I could only stay in there a few seconds before I became hysterical. When I got outside, the officers tried to comfort me. They thought what I had seen had upset me, and it had. But it was more the thought of what Jim had gotten himself into that tore me apart. These weren't bad people he was seeing. They were evil. And I knew they must want something from him, but I didn't know what." Carol looked over at Eric. "Do you know what it was?"

Eric shifted uncomfortable. "I can guess."

"Go ahead," Carol said. "It's already happened. It's done with."

"The girl Charlene needed your husband to be her victim in a ritual murder," Eric said.

"That can't be true," Alison blurted out. "Things like that don't happen now."

Carol shook her head sadly. "I'm afraid your friend is right. Charlene was an apprentice. She wanted to be a full-fledged witch. To be one she had to murder an innocent. Someone who loved her." Carol lowered her head, and a bitter tear trickled over her cheek. "That girl murdered my husband. She did it so that she could live forever."

"But how do you know that for sure?" Alison protested. "Did you talk to her? Did you see your husband again?"

Carol chewed on her lower lip, and her eyes were focused far away. "I didn't see him again, but I spoke to him once more on the phone. He called me at our house a couple of days later in the middle of the night. I had gone back to living there, by myself. The children stayed at my sister's. I hoped he'd come back. He sounded scared as he told me he was going to try to come home soon, but that he had some business to finish up first. He apologized for getting involved with Charlene. I asked him if he was in love with her, and he was silent for a long time and never did answer the question. Someone came into the room where he was, so he hung up. That was the last I heard from him."

"And did you ever speak to Charlene?" Alison repeated.

"No," Carol said. "But I spoke to her parents."

"Where?" Eric asked. "When?"

"At the morgue, when they came to identify Charlene's body."

"She's dead?" Alison asked.

Carol nodded grimly. "I hate to say it, but I'm glad. But let me back up and tell you what happened in the order it happened. The police set up a stakeout on the warehouse. But the cult must have got wind of it because they never went back there. I told the police about Charlene, but that's all I had—a first name and an incomplete description."

"Excuse me," Alison interrupted. "What color was Charlene's hair?"

"Blond," Carol said.

"Oh," Alison said thoughtfully.

"What is it?" Eric asked.

"Nothing," Alison said. "Please continue, Carol."

"The police couldn't find a missing young lady named Charlene. By that I mean there was no missing-person report on such a person. I went ahead and filed a missing-person report on Jim. I had the paper put in a small article about him. That was a waste. Then I had to sit and wait because nothing happened. Two weeks went by. I figured Jim was dead. Then one night I got a call from the police. They wanted me to drive to a hospital out in the San Bernardino Valley. They believed my description of Charlene matched a body that had been brought in."

"That's where I live," Alison said.

Carol nodded. "At the hospital *was* the body of Charlene—I recognized her. Her parents were there, too. Her real name was Jane and she had committed suicide by falling onto a propped-up knife in her own bedroom in the middle of the night, with black candles burning and pentagons painted in her own blood drawn all over her naked body. Her parents found her only a few minutes after she'd died. I can't tell you how distraught they were. And they didn't have good news for me.

"Jane had admitted to killing Jim before she did herself in?" Eric said.

"I should let you tell the story," Carol said.

"I'm sorry I keep interrupting," Eric said.

"I didn't mean that sarcastically," Carol replied. "You obviously have knowledge about these matters. I wish I'd had more—maybe my husband would be alive now. Anyway, you're right. Before her parents went to bed that night, Jane told them that she had killed her lover that night and dumped his body in the desert. She said it so matter-of-factly that they thought she was high on something. They told her to go to bed and sleep it off, whatever it was. Jane's parents had absolutely no idea their darling daughter was involved with Satanism, even though they knew she did drugs."

"What was the date you went to the hospital?" Eric asked.

"July twenty-eighth," Carol said.

Eric looked at Alison. "Was that the night of the concert?"

She thought a moment. "I think it was, yes."

"It must have been," Carol said. Her shoulders sagged with the weight of the memory. "Jane was the girl Jim had been with. I could see that with my own eyes, even as she lay on the cold slab in the morgue, naked, with a big bloody hole in her chest. And if Jane had just killed her lover, it had to mean Jim was dead. It was a relief in a way. I didn't have to worry anymore." Carol began to cry again. "I don't have to worry now."

Alison got up and went over to sit beside Carol and put an arm around her. She almost asked Carol if she had received any strange mail lately. But she figured Carol would have told them if she had. Alison wanted Carol to think it was over. The woman had suffered enough.

"That's my story," Carol said, and she hugged

144

Alison again. "I'm glad you found Jim's body as soon as you did. You didn't do me or my children a great injustice. We knew he was gone. I can understand how a group of kids could get scared and make the wrong decision. At least Jim wasn't left out in the open where animals could have messed with his body. You buried him deep, didn't you?"

"Yes," Alison. The grave hadn't been that deep. They'd had no tools and the ground had been hard. But she'd say anything to comfort the woman now.

Except for one big thing.

"Do you remember where you buried him?" Carol asked, wiping at her tears.

"I'm afraid not," Eric broke in. "We have no idea. We've tried to find the spot a dozen times and failed."

Carol frowned as she looked at him. "You were there that night, Eric?"

Eric paused. "No, I wasn't there. But I was made aware of what went on. Alison and I are old friends. I'm sorry we won't be able to reclaim your husband's body. But we would greatly appreciate it if you didn't go to the police with Alison's story. It could get the whole group in serious trouble, and there would be no point in it, not after all this time."

Carol nodded. She was a kind-hearted woman. "I understand. I'd like to be able to reclaim my husband's remains, but if it means hurting innocent people, then it's not worth it."

"We weren't innocent," Alison muttered shamefully.

"Mrs. Whiting," Eric began. "Would it be OK if I

asked a few blunt questions? Some of them might be painful for you."

Carol sniffed. "No, go ahead."

"Did Jane describe to her parents how she killed your husband?"

Carol's mouth quivered. "Yes. She said she pounded a sharp needle through the top of his skull while he was asleep."

"Did you see evidence of this on Jim's body?" Eric asked Alison.

"Not directly," Alison said. "But there was blood coming out of his mouth."

Eric considered. "A fine needle would hardly have spilt much blood." He returned his attention to Carol. "You mentioned that Jane believed that she would live forever once she made her ritual sacrifice. Why did you say that?"

"It was one of the things Jane told her parents before they went to bed," Carol said. "To them it was all babble. Jane said she was now ready for immortality."

Eric nodded. "Satan worshipers believe that when they've been fully initiated by their master, they will live a tremendously long life. Jane must have been convinced of the fact."

"But why, then, did she commit suicide?" Alison asked.

"She probably didn't think she'd die when she fell on the knife," Eric said. "Or rather, she probably thought she'd be reborn in her own body, with Satan's help and power. It's in the literature on cults. Murder and suicide are two of the gates into hell's power."

"Maybe there's something to the literature," Carol muttered.

"Why do you say that?" Alison asked.

"Because Jane's body disappeared from the funeral home before they could get it underground. I heard from the police." Carol forced a miserable laugh. "I'm not suggesting that she got up and walked away. The police believe other members of her cult came for the body to use in their ceremonies." The woman trembled. "It makes me sick to talk about things like this. She's dead, God save her soul. If it can be saved."

"Amen," Alison said.

They lapsed into silence. Carol was shrewd. She studied them as they sat digesting her gruesome tale. "Have any members of this cult been bothering you two?" she asked.

"We're not sure," Eric answered quickly. "It's possible. That's why we came here tonight to speak to you. Do you by any chance know how we could get in touch with Jane's parents?"

"I remember their name and the city they lived in," Carol said. "But I never asked them for their address. It wasn't like I wanted to keep in touch with them. They were Mr. and Mrs. Clemens and they lived in Riverside. Information might have their number."

Eric glanced at Alison. "We should probably go and leave Mrs. Whiting alone."

Alison nodded and stood. "It's getting late."

Carol got up anxiously. "If any member of that cult is bothering you, I suggest you go to the police immediately. These people have no consciences. They'll stop at nothing to get what they want."

"What do you think they want?" Alison asked.

Carol looked her straight in the eyes. "People's souls." Then the woman grimaced. "I just pray to God they didn't get my husband's."

*"Dying is not so bad as being put in the box."*

"I'll pray with you," Alison said.

# CHAPTER FOURTEEN

*E*ric was anxious to go straight to the Clemenses' house. He had been able to obtain their address from Information. But Alison insisted they stop and check on Brenda. Her best friend had been in a bad state at the end of the meeting at the park. Alison asked Eric to wait in the car while she ran inside. There was a single light showing in Brenda's window. The rest of the house was dark. The time was a few minutes before midnight. Alison let herself in without knocking. She had done so many times before.

Brenda was lying flat on her back with the music on low when Alison peeked in her room. Brenda glanced over with dreamy bloodshot eyes. There was a half-empty fifth of Seagrams 7 on the night table beside Brenda's head. Brenda seldom got drunk, but when she did, she favored whiskey.

"Ali," Brenda mumbled. "Is that you?"

"It's me." Alison crossed the room and knelt on the floor by her side. "How are you doing?"

Brenda looked at the ceiling and snorted softly. "How am I doing? Just great. They're bringing back what's left of Kipp tomorrow. His mom called and asked if I could help her pick out a casket for him. Can you imagine that? Two weeks ago I went with her to pick out a pair of pants for him." She began to cry, slurring her words. "Now I have to pick out a box to put him in."

Alison hugged her. "I know. It just keeps getting worse and worse. But Eric and I have been busy. We went and spoke to the man's wife. We have a lead on the people who might be behind the chain letters."

But Brenda wasn't interested. "We don't want to mess with that Caretaker. We better do what he says and let him put us in his box, and then maybe he'll go away and leave us alone."

"That's a lousy attitude."

"It's a smart attitude if you're into self-preservation." Brenda winced in pain. A bead of sweat poured off her forehead. "I need another drink." She reached for the bottle with her left hand, although her right hand was closer. Alison snapped the bottle away from her.

"You've had enough to drink," Alison said. "Go to sleep. I'll come see you in the morning."

Brenda persisted in wanting the bottle, although she was too drunk to jump up and take it back. She stuck out her left hand farther. "Just give me the goddamn bottle, Ali," she said.

Alison thought it was weird that Brenda was using her left hand. She was right-handed, like the rest of them. A warning bell went off in the back of Alison's head. She reached down and pulled away the sheet.

Brenda's right hand was covered with a bandage.

A red bandage. The blood was soaking into the top of the bed.

It looked as if she was missing her right index finger.

"Brenda!" Alison cried. "How could you do that to yourself?"

Brenda sat up, her face a mask of fury and fear. "How could I save my life? It wasn't hard. I got drunk enough and got a knife that was sharp enough and cut it off. Then I put the finger in an envelope with the chain letter and—"

Alison pressed her hands over her ears. "Stop it!"

"And I brought it over to Joan. That's what the ad said to do—give it to Joan. I couldn't have mailed it anyway. I put it in a plastic Baggie, but the blood soaked through the envelope anyway."

Alison felt nauseous. "You didn't have to do it."

Brenda grabbed her arm with her left hand. "The hell I didn't! I tell you this Caretaker isn't human. He goes where he wants. He does what he wants. You saw what he did to Kipp. What would he have done to me? Sawed me up into little pieces? It was better to lose just one piece and have it done with."

Alison shook her head miserably. "But you're in his box now."

"Who cares about his goddamn box?"

*"But it's difficult to get out once you are inside. Most people never do."*

"One day you might care," Alison said sadly. "I hope that day never comes for you. Can I take you to the doctor?"

Brenda glared at her. "I can drive with one hand."

"I think you should wake up your parents."

Brenda snickered. "And show them what I've done? That'll go over great. No, I think I'll wait until morning. When I'm sober. That's when I'll begin to feel the pain." More tears streamed over her face. "I miss Kipp."

Alison couldn't hug her again, and she didn't know why. Maybe it had something to do with her bloody finger. Maybe it was because she thought Brenda—

*Was already damned?*

When Neil had sent out his chain letters, the tasks he had assigned had each been personally distasteful to the recipient. These new tasks seemed to follow a similar pattern, except each task was personally damning. Fran had loved her puppy more than anything. Kipp had loved his sister more than anybody. And Brenda loved herself, her body—she was incredibly vain. But her vanity had now taken a serious blow. For the rest of her life she would be disfigured.

"I have to go" was all Alison could say. She set the bottle of whiskey down and left Brenda crying.

Eric was waiting impatiently in the car. He wanted to go to the Clemenses'. But when Alison told him what had happened, he thought they should go to Joan's house first. He was concerned that the Caretaker had broken his own pattern. He now wanted the letters brought to the next person.

"It's a small change," Alison said.

"Yes. But he may be trying to accelerate the cycle," Eric said.

"Why?"

"I don't know." He stared straight ahead out the car

window. The nighttime sky was ablaze with white light. "It's a full moon tonight. Maybe it has an occult significance for the Caretaker."

"Do you believe the Caretaker is connected to this Satanic cult Carol described?"

"I honestly do," Eric said. "The tasks listed in the paper have all had a ritualistic torture quality to them." He grimaced. "Brenda really cut off her finger?"

"It looked like it. But let's not talk about it." She tapped on the dashboard. "Let's drive. Let's go see Joan."

But Joan wasn't home, and they only succeeded in waking Joan's father, who was in a grumpy mood. Mr. Zuchlensky was a big, tough man who wasn't to be messed with. He stood in the doorway in his shorts, with his hairy stomach sticking out.

"Which one are you?" he demanded.

"I'm Alison Parker," Alison said. Eric was still in the car. "I'm the one your daughter can't stand."

He grunted. "You're the one who stole her boyfriend away, right?"

"He was never her boyfriend. She just thought he was. But I'm not here to argue about it. Do you have any idea at all where Joan went?"

"Nah. She was here until that other girl came over. What's her name?"

"Brenda?"

"Yeah, that's the one. She came over here with her hands wrapped in a towel. What a kook. Joan left right after her."

"Did she take anything with her when she left?"

153

"Not that I know of. I didn't actually see her. I was watching the news. That was tough what happened to those two friends of yours. I was sorry to hear about them."

Alison began to turn away. "Thanks, Mr. Zuchlensky. I'm sorry I woke you."

"It's all right. You try to stay out of trouble, you hear?"

"Yeah. Sure."

Alison noticed that the little metal door on Zuchlensky's mailbox at the end of the driveway was lying open.

Eric and Alison were at odds about where they should go next. He still wanted to talk to the Clemenses. She wanted to check on Tony. She was worried that Joan had gone to Tony's house—bearing strange gifts. She thought she was being logical. Tony didn't live that far from Joan. The Clemenses lived all the way out in Riverside, closer to her house. But Eric was insistent.

"He's probably not at home," Eric said as he restarted the car.

"Are you saying that he's with that girl?" she asked, hurt.

"I'm saying we need more information before we confront Tony. The Clemenses can give us that information."

"But he could be in danger."

Eric ignored her. He was heading for the freeway.

"Dammit, Eric, you saw that he spit on me today. That's not the Tony I know. That witch has done

154

something to his mind." She tried to grab the steering wheel. "I love him! I'm not going to let him die!"

Eric pushed her aside and quickly pulled over to the side of the road. He sat breathing deeply for a minute. He must be furious with her. She had almost yanked them into the oncoming traffic.

"I'm sorry," she said.

He sighed. "Alison, has it ever occurred to you why you might not be at the bottom of the list?"

She frowned. "We've talked about it."

"Not really." He reached out and put his hand on her knee. "It could be that the Caretaker knows you won't be around when he gets that far."

She was incredulous. "Are you saying that Joan's going to kill me?"

Eric shook his head and put the car back in gear. "I'm saying that it could be worse than you think."

It took them almost an hour to drive to the Clemenses'. They went to the door together. Alison didn't understand how people could continue to live in the same house where their daughter had impaled herself on a knife. She felt creepy walking up to the front porch.

Eric had to knock on the door for a long time to get an answer. Finally an elderly man appeared and peered at them through the torn screen. The Clemenses lived in a poor section of town and were obviously of modest means. Alison decided it had to be the same house Jane had died in. The man's bathrobe seemed to be in as poor shape as the screen.

"Can I help you?" he asked.

"Yes," Eric said. "We're here to talk to you about the group your daughter Jane was involved with. They've been causing us trouble, and it's important that we find out everything we can about them."

"Who are you?" the man asked.

"We're a couple of scared kids," Alison interrupted. "Please, Mr. Clemens, we know it's weird stopping by like this in the middle of the night. But we need your help."

"Did you know Jane?" the man asked.

"No," Alison admitted. "But we know of her. We know how she died. We know the man she killed before she died."

The man trembled at her remarks. "She wouldn't have hurt anyone before she got involved with those monsters." He opened the door for them. "Come on in. You both look decent. If I can help you, I will."

"Have we woken Mrs. Clemens?" Alison asked as she and Eric stepped inside. There was a muskiness to the house that Alison found distasteful. She glanced down the short narrow hallway as Mr. Clemens padded into the living room and took a seat. Jane's room must be down there, she thought. A chamber of horrors. How many times had the Clemenses sat in their quiet living room while Jane got loaded in her room and played music from Black Sex and painted pentagrams on her floor with cats' blood?

"There is no Mrs. Clemens," Mr. Clemens said. Sitting in the light of the living room, he looked close to sixty. They must have had Jane late in life, or perhaps she was adopted. "My wife died shortly after Jane."

Eric sat near Mr. Clemens, with his left ear toward the man. Alison had noticed that Eric relied on sight almost as much as his "better" ear to understand what people were saying.

"May we ask how she died?" Eric asked.

"She was in Jane's room one night dusting. I never went in there myself. I couldn't bear the memories. She let out a single scream and was lying dead on the floor when I got to her." Mr. Clemens shrugged. "The doctor said it was a heart attack."

"It must be hard for you living here all alone," Alison said.

Mr. Clemens coughed painfully. He sounded ready to have a heart attack himself. "It's hard," he agreed quietly. "Who told you Jane killed a man?"

"Mrs. Carol Whiting," Eric said.

Mr. Clemens twitched. "The poor woman." He paused. "What can I tell you?"

"The name of any of Jane's friends who might have been involved in the cult with her?" Eric asked.

"Jane didn't have any friends," Mr. Clemens said simply. "She was a loner. She was pretty as pie, but boys didn't ask her out. Girls didn't call her up. I never understood why. I don't understand now. I think if she had had a few decent friends, her life might have taken a different course." He paused again. "But that wasn't to be."

"She must have had somebody she talked to?" Alison said.

"Sure, she did," Mr. Clemens said, and there was bitterness in his voice. "The people in that cult. But I don't know any of their names. I don't want to know any of them."

Eric and Alison looked at each other. Had they hit a dead end already? Jane Clemens was their only lead. But then Alison glanced past Eric and Mr. Clemens to a cluster of family pictures standing on a dusty shelf at the top of an old bookcase. She couldn't make out much detail from where she sat, but a flash of green in the photograph of a young woman's eyes caught her attention.

Alison stood and slowly crossed the room. Suddenly she felt as if she were walking through a space where the normal laws of reality no longer applied. The red and purple lights of her nightmares flashed in her mind. The horrible smells and the crushing despair. They surrounded her as she walked across the simple living room of a poor man living in Riverside, California.

She reached the cluster of family photos.

She picked up the one of the beautiful girl with the green eyes. The eyes that shone like polished emeralds. Like a cat's eyes. Alison didn't have to ask. She knew intuitively that the photograph had been taken after Jane Clemens was already involved in the cult. Jane's eyes were bright, but the light they put out was as cold as the black water at the bottom of a well. Jane was blond, Mrs. Whiting had been right about that. But who was to say Jane couldn't dye her hair later in life?

Like, say, after she was dead?

Dye her lovely blond hair a deep, dark maroon.

Maroon—the color of the girl's hair in Tony's car.

The faces were the same. Identical. Jesus help them.

Dear dead Jane Clemens was sleeping with Alison's boyfriend.

"Oh, God," Alison moaned. She dropped the photograph, and the glass caught the edge of the bookcase and shattered in many pieces. Eric was at her side in an instant. It was a good thing. Alison felt the room spin and go dark, but Eric caught her before she could fall.

"What is it?" he demanded, holding her upright in his arms.

"It's her," Alison whispered.

"Who's her?" Eric asked.

Alison had to take a deep breath. She opened her eyes, and Eric helped her into a chair. Jane Clemens's picture had fallen facedown on the floor. Alison nodded for Eric to pick it up.

"It's her," she repeated.

"You've met Jane before?" Mr. Clemens asked from his seat on the other side of the room.

Eric picked up the photographs and shook the glass off. "Who is this?" he asked.

"You didn't get a good look at her this afternoon," Alison said. "I did."

"What are you talking about?" Eric asked.

"Jane is the same girl who was in Tony's car," Alison said.

"Hold on just a second," Mr. Clemens said, and he

was angry. "My daughter has been dead for over a year."

"I saw her today," Alison said firmly. "She's back."

Mr. Clemens stood and waved his hand in disgust. "I want you people to leave. Now."

"Alison," Eric began. "I don't think this is the time to be mixing people up. Mr. Clemens was nice enough to invite us into his—"

"I tell you I saw her!" Alison shouted. "She's dyed her hair, but it was her. I would recognize those eyes anywhere. Listen to me, both of you, Jane killed James Whiting as part of an elaborate ritual to gain physical immortality. Her body vanished from the mortuary. Mrs. Whiting said it in jest, but I think it was true, I think Jane got up and walked out of that mortuary."

Eric took Alison by the hand. "I'm sorry about this, Mr. Clemens. She's had an upsetting last few days. I'll take her home. Thanks for your time." He practically pulled her toward the door. "Goodbye."

"She's alive!" Alison called back toward the old man. "I think she's the one who gave your wife a heart attack!"

If Mr. Clemens answered, Alison wasn't given a chance to hear it. Eric had yanked her out the door, down the steps of the porch, and onto the sidewalk. He was angry, but so was she. She shook him off when he stopped beside her car. She had been letting him drive it all day.

"You have no right to drag me around like I was your dog!" she shouted at him.

"And you have no right to scream at a brokenhearted old man that you have just seen his daughter who's been dead for over a year!" Eric shouted back.

"She isn't dead! She's alive!"

"Jane Clemens was seen lying naked in a morgue with a huge hole in her chest!"

"Then she's come back from the dead! All I know is I saw her this afternoon! She's the Caretaker! She's the one who's sending us these chain letters!"

Eric quieted. "You don't know what you're talking about."

Alison also calmed down. She glanced up and down the block. The houses were all old and shabby. In the bright moonlight they looked like cardboard shacks. They were alone on the street. Their solitude sank deep into Alison's soul. Was there no one who could help them out of this nightmare? Satanic sacrifices and now the walking dead. And the chain kept going, from one link to the next.

*"A chain. An unbroken chain. It's very ancient—not a happy thing. But it can be broken."*

How? *With love* was all he would say.

The guy she loved was in the enemy's camp. But she had felt love in the stranger's presence in the mountains. It had been a beautiful thing. Sweet and innocent, free of all blemishes. It had been unworldly.

And yet it had been familiar. As familiar as the guy himself.

Where had she seen him before?

Why had she driven to that particular place?

Alison strained to remember back to the day after Neil died. The day she and Tony had gone for a walk near her house. The first day they had been sure it was all over. Tony had said something to her that was important. But what? Try as she might she couldn't . . .

Then Alison had it.

*"We went to the mountains. It was a pretty place, next to a lake. Neil liked it. I used my parents' credit card and rented a cabin. . . . We stayed there the whole week. . . . The Caretaker, the man, all that garbage was gone. We didn't even talk about it. . . . Mainly we just sat by the lake and skimmed rocks and that was good. I fixed him up this old cushiony chair next to the water, and he was comfortable enough. . . . He was sitting in it yesterday morning when he died."*

She had driven to the spot where Neil had died! Tony had talked about the place later, in more detail. She had known how to get there subconsciously. And she had gone right there when things had looked the darkest. Why? Because she knew she'd get help? Who had helped her?

*"I am your friend. I am your greatest admirer."*

Tony had described Neil as her greatest admirer.

After Neil's first funeral.

Neil had been buried a couple of times.

But had two times been enough?

Alison knew now who the guy at the cabin reminded her of.

Neil. It *had* been Neil, and yet someone else, too.

Another form of Neil Hurly.

Like Tony's girlfriend was another form of Jane Clemens.

*Oh, God, it just keeps getting worse.*

"Did you hear me, Alison?" Eric said.

Alison came back to the sidewalk as if from a million miles. She grabbed ahold of Eric. "We have to go out to the desert where we buried the man," she said.

"Why?"

"Because Neil told me I had to go there. He said I had to go back to where it all began. That's where it really all started. We have to dig up the man's grave and see if Neil's body is buried there."

"When did Neil tell you that?"

"You don't want me to answer that."

"But you said Tony buried Neil in the man's grave in the desert. What makes you think Tony was lying?"

"I don't think Tony was lying. I just think Neil's body might have disappeared."

"Why?"

Alison looked up at the full moon. She was confident she would be able to find the place. And they would have plenty of light to work by. "For the same reason Jane Clemens's body disappeared," she said.

# CHAPTER FIFTEEN

*T*ony dreamed of the inside of the box. But it was only a metaphor—his unconscious wrestling with the impossibility of it. Because the box was unimaginable to mortals. No one who went in it returned to tell of the tale. Or so they said.

*They.* The Caretakers.

Tony was inside a metal box that was approximately the size of his own room. This made sense because his physical body was actually lying asleep in his bedroom. But his soul was sweating. He was locked in a seamless metal jail that was suspended in a caldron of flames.

There seemed no way out.

But that was a lie. Everything that happened in the box was a lie.

He was so hot. He paced from featureless wall to featureless wall, and as the temperature steadily increased, he began to scream for help. It was then that Brenda suddenly appeared in one corner of the metal room. He had no idea where she'd come from. She carried a long silver knife.

"Brenda!" he cried. "What are you doing here? Do you know how to get out of here?"

She handed him the knife and stared at him with whiteless eyes—twin black marbles in a flat face. "Oh, Tony," she said. "We just have to open our hearts. That's what they all say, you know."

"Then we can leave here?" he asked.

She flashed a fake grin. He wished her eyes would return to normal. He didn't know what the hell was wrong with them. "Sure. Then we can leave together," she said.

"Who are they?" he asked, although he believed he knew the answer to that question.

"It doesn't matter," she said, wiping away a bead of sweat that actually looked more like a drop of blood. He noticed for the first time that her hands were bleeding and that she was missing several of her fingers.

"What happened to your hands?" he asked.

"I don't know," she said. "Let's just get out of here. We can talk about it later. It's hot!"

He turned the knife over in his hand. "What am I supposed to do with this?"

"Open our hearts, Tony baby." She ripped open her blouse. He could see her bra. It was a mess. She had splattered blood on it from her severed fingers. She pointed to the center of her chest. "Just stick it right here, and I can forget this place," she said.

"You mean, you want me to kill you?" he asked, horrified.

"It's not that way, Tony. You just have to open my heart. It's a simple operation. Go ahead, I don't mind." She reached for his hand with the knife in it. "Please hurry."

"No," Tony said, aghast. He pulled his hand away. "There must be another way."

Brenda's face suddenly became ugly. The change was dramatic. Her flesh actually took on lines and wrinkles that made it look like a witch's mask. Her voice came out high and cruel.

"You cut out my heart, or I'll cut out yours, little boy," she snapped. Magically another knife appeared in her hand, one longer than his. She stabbed at him, and Tony dodged to the side. Instinctively he slashed back with the knife she had given him. His aim proved true. He caught her in the center of her rib cage. The blade sunk in all the way to the hilt, and he felt warm fluid gush over his hand. Brenda's face relaxed, turning to normal. But a mess of blood bubbled out of her mouth as she sank to her knees in front of him.

"That hurts," she gasped in surprise as she died.

Tony looked down at the bloody knife in his hand.

He couldn't believe he had just killed someone. A friend at that.

He couldn't understand why it felt so good.

Then he was outside the metal box. He was floating in the abyss of red and purple lights, loud throbbing, and choking fumes. As before, he was closing on the vast dark wall. A huge black portal grew larger before him, and he felt himself being sucked inside. The lights vanished and all was silent. Once more he saw a slice of a bedroom, held up against a starless void. He moved steadily into the scene, and soon the room was all that existed. Yet the memory of where he had just come from stayed with him, and it was enough to terrify him.

He was in Neil's bedroom, and Neil was trying to screw up the courage to call Alison and ask her out. Tony watched as Neil dialed the number twice and then immediately hung up. Finally, on the third try, Neil was able to stay on the line long enough to have Alison pick up.

"Hello," Neil said. "Alison? This is Neil Hurly. How are you doing? That's great. I'm doing fine, thanks. The reason I called—I was wondering if you would like to go to a movie with me this Friday? Oh, you're busy. That's OK. How about Saturday? You're busy then, too? That's OK. How about next weekend? Oh, I see. Yeah, I know how that is. Well, I just thought I'd give you a call. Goodbye, Alison."

"Wait a second!" Tony yelled as Neil started to put down the phone. He strode across the room and snapped the receiver out of Neil's hand. "Let me talk to her." Tony raised the phone to his ear and mouth. "Hello, Alison? This is Tony. Would you like to go out to the movies this Friday? You would? That's great. When should I pick you up?" Alison gave him a time, and he hung up. He turned back to Neil. "See, that's the way to do it, buddy. You just be me, and everything goes perfectly."

But Neil wasn't listening. He'd already stood and begun to walk out the door. But he turned at the last moment and sadly shook his head at Tony. Tony wasn't sure what he had done wrong, other than steal his best friend's girl.

Then Tony was back in the metal room—in the box.

Alison was standing before him. She had a silver knife in her hand.

It was murderously hot inside the box.

"Tony," Alison said sweetly. "You've really opened my heart to what love is all about." Then she raised the knife and tried to stab him in the chest. But he was ready for her tricks. Brenda's witch had taught him well. He dodged to the side and managed to trip Alison. She fell forward and landed on her own knife. She rolled over on her back, and he saw that the blade stuck straight up out of the center of her chest. There was blood everywhere, especially in her hair. It gave her black curls a special maroon color. She smiled up at him, and blood gurgled out the sides of her mouth.

"Fooled you, didn't I?" she said, and her voice was different from Alison's. He realized it was Sasha who was lying on the floor in front of him. He watched in amazement as she yanked the knife out of her chest and tossed it aside. She reached up, and he helped her to her feet. She brushed her hands off on her black pants, but the blood didn't go away.

"I thought you were Alison," he said, confused.

"They always think that," Sasha said. She took his hand again. "Come. It's time. We have to go."

He took her hand reluctantly. This last murder had not felt so good as the first. He could have sworn it had been Alison in the room with him.

"Where are we going?" he asked.

She smiled. "They always ask that."

"Who are they?" he asked.

She laughed. "You are they. We are they. It makes no difference where we're going." She leaned over and whispered in his ear. "Soon you'll be in the box."

"But I thought this was the box," he said. It felt hot enough to be the box.

She giggled. She couldn't stop giggling. The sound of it began to make him feel sick. "Oh, no," she said finally. "This place is only to warm you up. You have no idea what the box is like."

Then she took his hand and led him away—to the other side of the wall. And soon the screams he heard were his own, and they never stopped.

Tony awoke and stared at his own ceiling. He turned over in bed and saw Sasha curled up in a ball beside him. She slept like a cat, he thought. He swung his legs off the side of the bed and sat up. His mouth was dry, and he had a headache. He must be getting sick. His entire body was soaked with sweat.

He stood and walked to the window and looked out at the deserted nighttime street. It looked like an alien planet. He didn't even feel he belonged in his own body. He hurt all over. He had gone to bed early only to awake at midnight and find Sasha standing over him. Before he could speak she had pressed her finger to his lips and whispered in his ear that she wanted his love. She had slipped into the bed beside him, and they had done the nasty deed, and it *had* been nasty. He had never experienced such passion with Alison, but it had taken its toll. He had passed out almost immediately afterward. Once more Sasha had refused to undress completely. She had kept her black blouse on. Indeed, she still had it on. It was the only thing.

Studying her sound asleep on his bed, Tony felt a sudden digestive spasm. The contents of his stomach welled up in his throat. He barely made it to his bathroom. He vomited up everything he had eaten for dinner and then some. He was catching his breath when Sasha came and knelt by his side. She leaned over and kissed him hard on the lips, vomit breath and all. She patted him on the back.

"Is my darling not feeling well?" she asked.

"I had a nightmare," he mumbled. It was just coming back to him. "I think it made me sick."

"What was it about?"

"I don't want to talk about it."

She grinned. Even in the unlit bathroom her green eyes glittered. He was reminded of the dead man in the desert. Of course, his green eyes had been flat as the ground he had been lying on.

"But I want you to talk about it," she said. "You will talk about it."

He smiled with her, although he felt far from smiling. "I have no choice in the matter?" he asked.

She continued to stare at him. Another wave of nausea swept through his body. "No," she said.

It was one little word. *No.* He had heard it a million times in his lifetime. But he had never heard it spoken the way she had just said it. There was a power in her voice that pushed a button deep inside him, one he didn't know he'd had. Maybe he hadn't had it until she'd come over that night. Their lovemaking had been passionate, but he couldn't say he'd enjoyed it. One of the reasons he felt sore was that she had scratched his back so badly in the throes of love.

Like a cat.

Her green eyes, green even in the dark, continued to hold him.

He told her about his nightmare. He remembered it all.

When he was done, she seemed happy. She patted him on the back again. Then she said something that shocked him to the core.

"Did I tell you I met Neil?" she said.

"What? No. When?"

"I met him in the desert where you buried the man. He had brought flowers to put on the man's grave. It was two months after you killed the man with your car, Tony."

"It wasn't my car," Tony said.

Sasha smiled. "But you were driving. You were responsible. Neil told me the whole story. I made him. He sounded so sad. I wanted to do something for him." She leaned closer. "Do you know what I did for him?"

Tony could not imagine. Everything she said blew his mind, which was already pretty well blown. "No," he said.

She moistened her lips with her tongue. Once more he smelled her smell. It wasn't really a hospital odor at all. He had just thought that because she had told him it was. But he was beginning to understand she didn't always tell him the truth. For some reason he was reminded of biology class in high school.

"I kissed him," she said.

His stomach rumbled. "Why?"

"I kissed him to make him feel better. I kissed his head. I kissed his knee. Do you remember he had a sore knee?"

"Yeah. He had a bone tumor in his leg. He ended up with a brain tumor. That's what killed him." Of course, Neil had not had these tumors two months after the incident in the desert. He had only developed them later.

"He was in a lot of pain," Sasha said sympathetically. "I made him feel better. He needed a friend. He felt awful about what you had done to the man. I talked to him regularly about it." She chuckled. "I talked to him even when he didn't know I was talking to him."

*"But this thing got in my head, and I couldn't get rid of it. I don't know where it came from. It was like a voice. . . ."*

"Did you know about the chain letters?" Tony asked, shocked.

"I know many secrets." Sasha sat back on her heels. "I kissed Neil, and now I've kissed you. But I've done more for you than give you a kiss, and now you'll do more for me than even Neil did." She cocked her head to the side. "I believe we have a visitor."

He could hear nothing. "What are you talking about? What did Neil do?"

"Shh," she said. "Listen. There it is. Someone's here."

She was right. Someone was knocking softly on the front door. He stood and grabbed his robe and hurried downstairs. Sasha didn't follow him. He opened the door, half expecting to find Alison. But it was Joan. She carried a brown paper sack in her right hand.

"Hi," she said flatly. "I have something for you." She thrust out the bag. "Take it. Do what you want with it. I'm sorry I'm late with it. I had to—go somewhere first before I could bring it over."

He took the bag reluctantly. "What's going on here?"

Joan spoke like a robot. "Brenda brought me her chain letter. She did what she was told to do. I'm doing what I was told to do."

"Who told you?" Tony asked.

"There was a note in my mailbox. One for me, one for you. Yours is in the bag, with the gun."

"What gun? What do I need a gun for?"

"It's my father's. Read the Caretaker's note. You're going to need everything I gave you."

Sasha suddenly appeared at Tony's side. Joan's eyes widened when she saw her, and she took a step back. Sasha grinned a mouth full of teeth.

"Is it loaded, Joany?" Sasha asked.

Joan swallowed. "I know you," she said.

"You're going to know me better," Sasha said. "You've done what you were supposed to do."

Joan trembled. She stammered. "I didn't hurt anybody."

Sasha laughed. "You just keep telling yourself that. Get out of here, worm. I'll come for you later." Sasha shut the door in her face. She turned to Tony. "Open the bag."

Tony searched inside the bag. If he hadn't just thrown up, he would have done so then. Joan had brought her dad's gun, all right. It could even have been loaded—he hadn't checked. Joan had brought it over with the trigger pulled back.

With a bloody severed finger.

"Brenda," Tony breathed. The gun fell from his hand onto the floor. It was fortunate it didn't go off. The finger bounced loose. Sasha reached down and retrieved them both. She pocketed the finger and flipped open the revolver chamber. It was fully loaded.

"It's hers," Sasha cackled. "Oh, Tony, we are going to have fun tonight. Hurry, read your small service. I'm going to help you perform it."

Tony reached into the bag again and withdrew a crumpled purple paper. He read in the shaft of white moonlight that shone through the window beside the front door. He didn't have to decode it.

Blow Alison's brains out.

He dropped the note in horror. "I can't do that."

Sasha was amused. "Why not? Do you know what your dear Alison is doing right now? She's on her way with her new boyfriend to dig up Neil's body. She's going to turn it over to the police. She's going to put you in jail, Tony."

Tony put his hands to his ears. "Stop it! She wouldn't do that to me!"

"She's doing it as we speak." Sasha pulled his hands down and placed the revolver back in his palm. "You're going to have to kill her. If you don't kill her, she'll destroy you."

"But, Ali—"

"Is a whore," Sasha said, sweeping in closer so that she was practically whispering in her ear. But the funny thing—he wasn't sure if she was speaking at all. It seemed as if her thoughts were simply inside his head. That they were the same as his thoughts. Yes, that was the way of it.

*"She's a whore, and she's spent the night screwing her new boyfriend and laughing about what an asshole you are. Now she's digging up Neil's body so that she can put you in jail so that she can screw anybody she wants while you rot away."*

"Is this true?" Tony whispered, standing frozen in shock. This new voice was a revelation to him. It knew so many secret things. It had been there for months, he suddenly realized. Ever since Neil had died. It was funny how long it had taken for him to hear it clearly.

Sasha kissed his ear, briefly sticking her tongue inside, and said, "It's all true, my love."

"I would have to see it for myself," he heard himself say.

"You will see it. I promise you. We will go there now."

*"You will see your whore digging in the mud, and you will take the gun and put a hole in her brain and bury her in the mud, and then you will be my love. We will make love on her grave, and it will be like heaven."*

He turned his head toward her and felt her tongue slide over the side of his face. Her eyes stared at him only inches away—twin mirrors hung in a featureless box. Her smell was overpowering—the stink of the morgue.

"Who are you?" he asked.

*"The Caretaker. The one who takes care of you."*

Sasha smiled. Her mouth did. But her eyes didn't change. They never did. They just watched. She was the Observer, the Recorder. She was also the Punisher. He had to listen closely. The time had come for his punishment. She brushed her hand through his hair.

"I'm your greatest admirer," she said.

# CHAPTER SIXTEEN

Alison found the spot without having to search. Even with the passage of time and the dark, there were still visible signs: tire tracks on the road that the winter's worst had failed to obliterate, scraped rubber on the asphalt that would probably be there at the turn of the century. But had there been no evidence, she would still have recognized the place where Tony had lost control of the car. For her, as well as for Tony, it was haunted, and her ghost, as well as the man's, often walked there at night. Alison and Eric parked their car, grabbed their shovels, and climbed outside.

"How far off the road did you bury him?" Eric asked. They wouldn't need flashlights. The moon shone in the sky like a cold sun.

"Fifty paces, straight out," Alison said. "Come on."

"What are we expecting to find?" Eric asked, following beside her as they strode through the sticky tumbleweeds. Alison remembered the night it all began—the howling wind, the dust in their eyes. That night the area was bathed in serenity—but it was as

false a peace as that achieved by suicide. They ha
given themselves a death sentence that night a yea
ago when they had tried to pretend to the world the
hadn't killed anybody. The irony of it all was that the
hadn't. The man had already been dead. If only the
had known!

"An empty grave," Alison said.

"But if we don't find anything, how can we be sur
we weren't digging in the wrong spot?" Eric asked.

"I'll know."

"But what will the empty grave prove?" he per
sisted.

Alison stopped. "I tell you I met Neil up in th
mountains."

"But you said he had terminal cancer. Even if Tony
lied about him dying, he would have died shortl
after."

"He's alive," she said. "He died and he came back."

"Alison, people don't come back to life. It's jus
fantasy."

She raised her eyes to the big round moon. She
thought of the enchanting love of the stranger. She
remembered the knives that had stabbed outwar
from the girl's eyes.

"Maybe they come back as something other than
people," she said.

A minute later they entered a small clearing in the
field of tumbleweeds and cacti. The latter stood
around them like frozen sentinels. They had counted
fifty paces, and here the soil was grossly uneven. It
should have been. Tony had buried Neil only two
months earlier.

"This is the spot," she said. "Neil's body should be right beneath us."

"I have to tell you I'm not looking forward to this," Eric said.

"It doesn't matter. You're already in this too deep." She pulled off her coat. The evening was cool, but she knew that soon she'd be sweating. "Let's get to work."

They had bought their shovels at an all-night grocery store and were lucky that the place had any shovels at all. But the quality of the shovels matched the quality of drugstore jewelry. A couple of feet into the ground and the wooden handles were coming loose from the metal spades. Eric muttered something about coming back later with better equipment, but Alison tossed a shovelful on his pants. Keep digging, brother.

The soil was a mixture of dirt and sand. It was not tightly packed—another sign that they had found the right spot. Working together they were down to five and a half feet in a hurry. Eric raised his shovel for another deep plunge. Despite his complaints, he was a hard worker, stronger than he looked. His spade stabbed into the earth, and it made a squishing sound.

As if it had plunged into something that had once been alive.

"Oh, Christ," he muttered. He was afraid to pull the shovel back out. He looked over at Alison, who had suddenly frozen in the moonlight at the sick sound. The two of them were standing head deep in the grave.

*Neil's body is still here. He didn't rise from the dead.*

Was she wrong about Jane Clemens as well?

An arm swung out of the night above them.

It struck Eric hard across the head, and he crum
pled at Alison's feet.

She screamed, then all at once her scream choked i
her throat.

Tony Hunt, her dearest love, accompanied by Jan
Clemens, witch from hell, appeared above her at th
edge of the grave. Tony was carrying a baseball ba
and a black revolver stuck out of his belt. He peere
down at her with eyes cold as Arctic frost. The gi
beside him giggled.

"We won't have to do any digging," she said. "We'l
just cover her over. Both of them." She turned t
Tony. "Do you believe me now?"

"It's true," he said softly, his voice void of an
inflection.

The girl raised her arms above her head, stretching
"Kill her now, Tony. It'll give us that much longer t
roll in the mud above her corpse."

Tony dropped the bat and pulled the revolver out o
his belt.

"Wait!" Alison cried. "Tony, listen to me. This gir
has lied to you. She's not who she says she is."

Tony aimed the gun at Alison. "I know that. Bu
you aren't who you say you are. You lied to me. You'r
a whore."

"No!" Alison pleaded. "I never cheated on you.
just gave Eric a quick hug and kiss good night. I woul
have done it right in front of you, and you'd neve
have minded. Tony! Don't kill me!"

"You did do it right in front of me," Tony sai
grimly. He cocked the revolver. "Say goodbye to life
Ali."

*"Say goodbye to life, Ali."*

The thought floated into Alison's mind like an echo from a shout in a canyon. But it wasn't her own thought. It came from the outside. She recognized that fact immediately because there was a harshness to it that pained her. She glanced up at Jane Clemens, who was posed above the grave as if she were being photographed for a men's magazine. Jane had Tony under some kind of mental control. Alison said the first thing that came to her mind, that belonged to her alone.

"Tony," Alison said. "She made Neil do things the same way she is making you do things. She's the Caretaker."

Tony's aim wavered. The mention of Neil threw him for a second. He blinked and looked around, seeming to discover for the first time where he was.

"Neil was the Caretaker," Tony said, confused.

"No," Alison said. "Neil was a pawn of the Caretaker. We've all been pawns. The girl standing beside you is the Caretaker. Look at her. Does she look human?"

Tony glanced at the girl. She ignored him at first. She stopped posing and moved around to the far side of the grave. She appeared unconcerned about Tony hesitating. Arrogance dripped from her every pore.

"You can climb out of the hole if you want, Ali," the girl said. "I won't kick dirt in your face."

Alison boosted herself out of the hole with difficulty. She brushed the dirt off her pants and stood upright. She was at the head of the grave, with the girl on her left and Tony on her right. Tony looked as if his plug had been pulled. For the moment the girl was not feeding him any evil thoughts. But Alison knew that moment wouldn't last.

Her shovel handle stood just below Alison's right foot. She must have set her shovel upright when Tony clobbered Eric.

"What's your plan, Jane?" Alison asked the girl.

The girl chuckled at the question. "I am not Jane. Jane is in the box. Jane will be staying in the box."

"Is that what you've planned for all of us?" Alison asked.

The girl gestured to Eric—almost invisible at the bottom of the hole—and at her. "You two are just props," she said. "You'll go no farther than this grave."

"But Tony?" Alison asked.

The girl sighed with exaggerated pleasure. "Ah, Tony. He's mine, all of him." She kicked a clod of dirt into the hole. "I'll take his body to places he's never imagined."

Alison shuddered. "Will he still be inside it?"

The girl nodded her approval. "Very good, Alison. You see the greater goal. Another Caretaker will come, and then another. An endless chain of them, you might say. There are so many of us who want to come out and play."

"And the chain letters?" Alison asked.

"An initiation process," the girl said. "It prepares people to welcome us into their hearts."

"By damning their souls," Alison said bitterly.

"Gee. That sounds impressive," the girl said, mocking.

"And if they don't get ready, they die?" Alison said.

The girl giggled. "There are worse things."

"The box," Alison said.

"You think you know about that," the girl said, and now the tone of her voice became serious, almost sad. "But you don't. None of you know." She was silent for a second, introspective, then she shook herself and laughed lightly. She gestured to Tony. "Kill her now, my love. Kill her slowly."

*"Kill her so that she suffers. Blow off bits of her at a time. I want to see her squirm like a wounded animal."*

Tony raised his gun as if he were a stringed puppet. The barrel of the revolver shone in the silver light of the moon. "Kill my love," Tony mumbled. Once more he cocked the hammer.

Then the girl let out a shout of surprise.

Alison twisted toward her to watch her topple into the hole.

Eric had grabbed the witch by the leg!

Tony's aim wavered. The dull, confused expression returned to his face as he watched his master fall into the grave. "Sasha?" he said.

Alison took advantage of the confusion. Bending down, she grabbed the top of the shovel handle and snapped it into her hands. Tony was just beginning to turn back to her when she let fly with a wide sweeping arc. The spade caught the tip of his revolver and sent it flying into the tumbleweed. Stunned, Tony turned to retrieve it. He must have been totally out of it. He didn't even see the blow coming that Alison delivered to the back of his skull. It sent him to the ground.

In the grave the girl was wrestling with Eric. She was winning. Eric let out a howl of pain as the girl stood up to climb out of the hole. Alison brought the shovel down on the top of her head, too. The girl grunted and fell backward.

Now what?

Alison realized she had done as well as she was going to do with one shovel. Both she and Eric had already lost the element of surprise. Tony was stunned, but recovering swiftly. She could whack him again, but she was afraid of doing him serious damage. The witch was already getting back up. Alison considered searching for the gun, but it would take her at least a minute to find it in the weeds. She glanced down at Eric. Whatever the girl had done to him, he wasn't going to be of any help in the next ten seconds. She had no choice, and she hated it. She had to take care of herself. She had to make a run for it.

Alison dropped the shovel and leapt across the grave. She took off for the car. The jagged tumbleweed tore at her legs, but she didn't let them slow her down. She ran as if she had the devil on her heels, and maybe she did. She had parked with the driver's side facing the gravesite. She was running so fast she did the majority of her braking by slamming into the car. Frantic, she threw the door open and jumped inside. But she didn't have her keys. Where were her keys? She couldn't remember. They were in her pocket. Yes! She stuck her hand in the pocket and pulled them out. But then she made the horrible mistake of sticking the wrong key in the ignition. She yanked it out and dropped the whole key chain to the floor.

Alison had just leaned over to find the keys when a fist came through the passenger window above her.

Shattered glass spewed over her. A hand like a claw grabbed her by the hair.

"Ouch!" Alison cried as she was yanked upright.

"Going somewhere?" the girl asked, standing just outside the window. Her grip on Alison's hair was enough to make Alison feel as if she were about to have the top of her skull ripped off. But the girl was not in the best of situations, either. She did, after all, have her arm stuck through a mean broken window. In fact her arm was already lacerated in a half dozen places.

But she wasn't bleeding. Instead, the cuts dripped a foul-smelling fluid. Alison had smelled the odor earlier in the day when Tony had spit on her. Then she had just caught a whiff of it. Now the stink of it flooded her nostrils.

Embalming fluid.

Jane Clemens had been embalmed before the Caretaker had taken possession of her body.

"Go to hell," Alison said. She jammed the right key in the ignition and turned it over. The girl tried tightening her hold on Alison's hair, but Alison was already slamming the car into gear. It jerked forward, and Alison felt a thousand hair roots yanked out of the top of her head. But flooring the accelerator had worked. The girl let go.

Oh, but the pain of losing so much hair at once. It sent such shock waves into Alison's central nervous system that she simply couldn't drive straight. The car raced straight forward but then immediately veered back off the road and got stuck. She had plowed into a mess of tumbleweed—sort of like Tony had done when he had gone off the road the summer before. Her head struck the steering wheel, and a black wave crossed her vision. But she didn't let herself faint. She threw the car in reverse and backed out of the wall of weeds. But as she flew backward she hit something hard—maybe a body. For a moment she had the horrible thought that she had run over Tony. She fretted between racing off and checking. The indecision cost her precious seconds. Finally she turned and glanced over her shoulder.

It was at that instant that the car door was ripped off its hinges.

The girl stood in the moonlight three feet to Alison's left, dripping embalming fluid from her crushed guts and grinning from ear to ear. There was a tire mark across her tattered black blouse. Alison saw how the girl could have survived the wreck with Fran. She must have been in the car with Fran, after all.

"You're a feisty devil," the girl said. "I like that."

She reached inside the car and grabbed Alison by the throat.

"Please," Alison croaked, but she was asking the wrong monster for mercy. The girl yanked her out of the car as if she were made of paper. She threw Alison in front of her, in the direction of the grave.

"Don't make me carry you," the girl warned.

Eric and Tony were waiting for them at the grave. Eric had recovered his wits, and Tony had found his gun. At the moment he had it pointed at Eric's head. The girl suddenly shoved Alison from behind, and Alison fell at Tony's feet. Dirt pushed into her mouth. Blood seeped over the side of her head from her clump of missing hair. She spit and looked up. Tony had the barrel of the gun pointed at her head.

"All right," she whispered. "I give up."

"Good," the girl cackled. "We are about to start carving you up anyway. It's a good time to give up."

Alison got up slowly. She didn't know how to reach Tony. She stared deep into his eyes and saw another person at work. She had felt this way once before, when talking to Neil in the throes of his madness. How had they gotten to Neil? With Fran. With the one girl in the whole world who loved him.

*"How can we break it?"*

*"With love?"*

*"I don't understand."*

Now she understood. Now she knew what to do.

She remembered her nightmares.

Tony could not be put in the box.

She loved Tony. She really did. It would be all right.

"Can I ask something before I die?" Alison asked.

"Of course," the girl said. "You can ask things *while* you're dying, if you can stop screaming. The night's young. We'll play a while before you go in the ground."

"You've got serious psychological problems," Eric told her.

"Yeah," the girl said. She poked Eric in the gut, and he doubled up in pain. "We'll play with you as well."

"Stop that!" Alison cried.

"I don't think so," the girl said.

"All this, from the very beginning, was to prepare us?" Alison asked.

"Yes," the girl said. "But I had to step in. I had to

get you to Column Three. Neil couldn't take you that far."

"Because Neil wouldn't," Alison said. "He had a good heart. He got away from you in the end."

The girl stared down into the grave. She spat out a mouthful of embalming fluid. "It doesn't look to me like he got very far."

"Tony," Alison said, turning to her boyfriend, and now she was crying. It was hard, what she had to do—so hard. She needed him to help her. "I can help you. Let me help you."

Tony blinked and a tremor went through the length of his body. "You lied to me," he said, but it was without force.

*"But beyond this you must trust what's in your heart."*

"This thing here lied to you," Alison wept. "It lies to you in your own mind. You have to listen to me with your heart. You know me in your heart, Tony. You put me in there and kept me safe and warm. You told me that once when we were alone together."

Tony fidgeted. He looked at the girl, then back at Alison. "You came here to get the body to bring to the police," he mumbled. "You turned against me."

"Yes," the girl said.

"No," Alison said. "I was always on your side. I'm on your side now." She took a step closer to him. The tip of the black barrel was practically touching her, pointed directly at her heart. "I love you. I'll always love you."

But even as she spoke the words, she knew it was no use. The girl stood at Tony's right, smirking. She was confident. No doubt she had fought similar battles over the course of centuries and always won. The stranger had said the chain was very ancient.

"Alison," Tony said, and there was pain in his voice but no strength. Alison knew it would take strength to break the chain. The strength that love gave.

Alison whipped her hand up and folded her fingers around Tony's right hand. His index finger was pressed to the trigger. She pressed it tight. Yes, it was *she* who pulled the trigger. Not her boyfriend.

Alison heard a loud roar. She felt a painful slap.

Then she was lying flat on her back, staring up at the sky.

Tony and Eric and the girl were peering down at her.

The girl looked more shocked than the guys.

"What did you do?" she asked in disgust.

Tony's face crumpled. "Alison?" he cried.

Alison smiled through her pain. "Tony."

"You witch!" Tony swore, turning on the girl. Before the girl could react, he pressed the gun to the side of her head and pulled the trigger. There was a flash of orange light. The girl toppled out of sight. Tony dropped the gun and knelt beside Alison. He reached out for her.

"What have I done?" Tony moaned.

"Don't move her," Eric cautioned Tony, trying to stop him.

"Let him take me," Alison whispered, and now the pain was coming in red tidal waves. She felt as if her chest had exploded, which it had. She could feel a mess of blood under her blouse, dripping down her belly. "I want to die in his arms."

Tony began to weep. "You're not going to die." He bit his lip and hugged her face to his shoulder. "Oh, God, what have I done?"

Alison was having trouble breathing. But she managed to smile. It felt good to be held by him again. "You didn't do anything. I did it. No one can put you in the box. You're free. You're—" It was difficult to get out the words. "You're mine."

Tony continued to hold her, but he shook them both as sobs racked him. He implored Eric, "Can't you do anything for her?"

Eric was sad. "There's nothing we can do."

Alison felt herself growing faint. The pain was receding into the distance. She closed her eyes, and Tony eased her back onto the ground. It was good to lie down and be still. It had been a long time since she had had a chance to rest. Now she could. She was at peace. She had done what had to be done. That was the best that anybody could do.

Far away, a million miles perhaps, she heard footsteps. Someone was approaching. But she couldn't get her eyes to open to see who it was. Yet she knew it was someone good, and she felt happy.

# EPILOGUE

*T*ony and Eric watched the stranger walk out of the dark with a mixture of awe and fear. He was nothing to look at—a slightly built guy with sandy brown hair and an innocent expression. Yet he walked with power. The white light of the moon shimmered around him. They rose as he stepped into their small circle.

"Who are you?" Tony asked.

The stranger didn't say anything for a minute. He just stared down at Alison as she lay dying on the ground. But his eyes—they were warm and green, somehow familiar to Tony—were not unhappy. Finally he looked at them.

"I am a friend," the stranger said.

"Can you help my girlfriend?" Tony asked. A stupid question. Nothing could help Alison now. Any fool could see she was dying.

"Your madness has passed," the stranger said. "You're all right now."

Tony nodded. His heart was broken, his girl was dying, but suddenly he felt lighter. The stranger spoke the truth—a great burden had been lifted from his shoulders. He looked down at the girl in disgust, a bundle of stinking fluid and blood lying beside the grave. He couldn't imagine how he had ever gone to her.

"I'm all right," Tony agreed. He gestured helplessly to Alison on the ground and began to cry miserably. "But Ali isn't."

The stranger seemed unconcerned. He stepped over to the fallen girl with the bloody head. Incredibly her ruined body had begun to stir. This didn't disturb the stranger, either. He stood over the grotesque heap until something began to worm its way out of the dead girl's mouth. It was black and slimy. It looked like a slug, but it was as big as a snake. The thing stuck its head into the nighttime air, then focused on Alison's dying figure. Suddenly it darted out of the girl's mouth, and its full length was revealed, more than five feet long. It dashed straight for Alison. But the stranger was too quick for it. He slammed his heel down on the head of the snake, crushing it. The thing rolled over in the mud and fell into the hole and was gone.

"Did you see that?" Tony gasped to Eric.

"No," Eric said.

"That thing that just came out of the witch's mouth," Tony said.

"I didn't see anything," Eric said, confused.

The stranger regarded both of them with calm. "This Caretaker is gone. It will not return. And Alison has passed a great test. She is ready for great things. There's no need to grieve over her. She'll be in good company soon." The stranger turned to walk back into the desert. "Goodbye, Eric. Goodbye, Tony."

Something in the way the stranger said his name touched Tony in a deep way. He *knew* that voice. It was the voice of a friend, the voice of *his* friend. But that was impossible, Tony told himself. They were standing beside the grave of that friend. He had buried the guy.

The stranger sounded like Neil.

Tony jumped at him, catching the guy by the hand just before he was out of their circle. "Neil!" Tony cried and threw himself to the ground at his feet. "Don't leave me. Don't let her leave me."

The stranger slowly turned and lay his hand on Tony's head. His touch was soothing beyond belief. Tony felt his sorrows melt beneath those magical fingers. But there were so many sorrows—and the stranger was in a hurry.

"Your friend has to go," the stranger said. "He only came back to offer what help was allowed. But it was enough. The chain is broken. Life will go on. Your life will continue." He patted Tony's head. "Be strong."

Tony could not be strong. He couldn't bear a future without Alison. "No. I want to go with you. I want to be with Alison, wherever she is. There's nothing for me here without you two." Tony kissed the stranger's hand. "Please? Let me go?"

The stranger slowly shook his head. "You're alive. You have to live. It is the way of things."

Tony stared into the stranger's face, and he could not remember when he had ever seen such love.

Alison had told him to listen to his heart, not his head. Well, deep inside he felt there was nothing that the stranger's love could not do.

"Heal her," Tony said. "Before she dies."

The stranger was silent for a moment. Then he raised his head to the stars. For a long time he stood like that, and if he breathed, he didn't show it. Finally he patted Tony on the head again. He smiled a playful smile.

"You want a miracle?" he asked.

"Yes!" Eric cried, coming over and joining them. "I would love a miracle. I've never seen one before."

The stranger laughed easily. Tony pressed the guy's hand to his forehead. "Please?" Tony begged.

The stranger took his hand back and knelt in front of Tony. He put both his hands on Tony's shoulders and bid Eric to come closer. "I'll tell you a secret," he said to both of them. "Joan took a long time to bring the gun to your house, Tony, because she first had to find blanks to fill it with. She never did the bidding of the Caretaker. She fooled the Caretaker."

Eric and Tony glanced back at Alison, and at the fallen girl. "But Alison is dying," Tony protested. "That witch is dead. The revolver must have been loaded."

Eric interrupted. "But, Tony, you pressed the revolver to the girl's temple when you pulled the trigger. Even if it was loaded with blanks, it could still have killed her. Most people don't know this, but blanks shoot out quite a formidable wad of paper. At high speed it can be lethal. The temple is the weakest part of the skull."

"But what about Alison?" Tony asked. "She's bleeding. She's dying."

"The same thing," Eric said. "She pressed the tip of the barrel flush with her chest. Even a blank would have torn up her skin pretty bad. But the wound shouldn't be fatal." Eric glanced at the stranger, who seemed to intimidate him. "Is that true?"

The stranger nodded. "It is the truth. See it how you wish it." He closed his eyes briefly before reopening them. "Alison can stay with you. That much is granted. It is all right." He stood. "Go to her. Take care of her. I am leaving now."

Tony reached out and shook the stranger's hand. He looked him straight in the eye, and this time the impact wasn't so overwhelming. Tony felt as if he were merely saying goodbye to an old friend.

"Will I see you again?" Tony asked.

"Someday," the stranger promised. Then he turned and walked into the night and was gone. Tony and Eric hurried over to Alison. She was still breathing. In fact, she appeared to be gaining strength. Tony helped her to a sitting position, and she opened her eyes.

"Am I dead yet?" she asked.

"No," Tony said. "You're going to be fine." He felt under her blouse in the area of her wound. Eric was right. Her flesh was badly torn, but the bleeding was slowing down. He applied pressure to the wound. He could not find a bullet hole. Yet he could have sworn when she was first shot— There had been that powerful recoil. . . .

"Is she going to live?" Eric asked hopefully.

"I think so," Tony said. "I honestly do."

Alison jerked in his arms, then relaxed. "I think so, too," she said. She smiled sheepishly at Tony. "Who was here?"

"I don't know," Tony said, raising his eyes to the brilliant moon. "A friend. Someone wonderful." He nodded to Eric. "Let's get her to a hospital."

Eric helped Tony lift Alison into his arms. As they walked back toward the car, Eric suddenly stopped. "I'd like to check the revolver and see if it really does have blanks in it," Eric said.

"You think maybe it didn't?" Tony asked.

"I just want to know for sure," Eric said, turning. Tony stopped him.

"Don't check," Tony said. "Let's see it how we wish it." He leaned over and kissed Alison on the forehead. She sighed and snuggled warmly into his arms. "To me it's a miracle," he said.

---

# Look For Christopher Pike's

*Master of Murder*

---

## About the Author

CHRISTOPHER PIKE was born in Brooklyn, New York, but grew up in Los Angeles, where he lives to this day. Prior to becoming a writer, he worked in a factory, painted houses, and programmed computers. His hobbies include astronomy, meditating, running, playing with his nieces and nephews, and making sure his books are prominently displayed in local bookstores. He is the author of *Last Act, Spellbound, Gimme a Kiss, Remember Me, Scavenger Hunt, Final Friends* 1, 2, and 3, *Fall into Darkness, See You Later, Witch, Die Softly, Bury Me Deep, Whisper of Death,* and *Chain Letter 2: The Ancient Evil,* all available from Pocket Books. *Slumber Party, Weekend, Chain Letter, The Tachyon Web,* and *Sati*—an adult novel about a very unusual lady —are also by Mr. Pike.